Safe in Eden

Alyssa Nowak

Safe in Eden

ISBN: 0692089551

ISBN-13:978-0692089552

1

CHAPTER ONE

The words echo through the small house from the living room television, "there has been a new development in the disappearance of Corey Dillon. A neighbor has come forward with information indicating violence within the household in the form of a loud fight the night of Corey's disappearance. Further investigation has led to Michael Dillon, Corey's father, being arrested for child abuse. Mr. Dillon continues to be a suspect in his son's disappearance. More on the story at six," The news anchor stated before breaking for a laundry detergent commercial.

"The little shit probably deserved whatever he got!" my father slurs loudly before opening another beer. It's only four pm and he is already drunk, that would be my cue to leave. I quietly slip on my old worn out black converse sneakers and hand-me-down blue hoodie. As I make my way through our musty living room, an empty beer bottle crashes against the wall next to my head. The shattering sound is piercing and makes my ears ring but I barely flinch anymore. At least his aim gets worse with each drink.

"Where the hell do you think you're goin?" He slurs, his appearance is sloppy and he is having a hard time keeping his eyes focused on me. I start picking up the bigger pieces of glass before responding.

"I am just going for a walk," I lie, it's not like he will be able to remember I even exist in a few hours anyway. The smell of beer makes my stomach turn as I finish cleaning up the broken bottle. I notice an empty bottle of vodka and about six empty beer bottles next to his worn out recliner. As he attempts to stand up but stumbles back again. The sudden shift in weight cases the old recliner to groan. I am moderately impressed that it hasn't broken yet. I hurry to the kitchen and hear him stumble attempting to get up again. I throw away the glass shards and wash the old beer off of my hands. I turn to dry my hands on the towel, left in a heap on the counter. He staggers into the kitchen swearing under his breath.

"You better not be seeing that Lee kid. My daughter don't need to be around them kind!" he has to hold himself up on the kitchen door frame just so he can manage to look at me and stand up at the same time.

He is referring to Lee Dimka who has been our neighbor and my best friend since we were six. The Dimka family was there for me more than my own father was. Unfortunately along with his drinking habits, he tends to see complexion before deeds. I dared not call him a useless racist even though I am thinking it, he has me cornered and it isn't worth getting hit over.

"It's just a walk dad, I will see you tonight" my statement is not a complete lie. I usually stayed out long enough for him to be out cold when I get home. He turns to the nearly empty fridge, probably for more beer. I see an opening and take it, ducking out past him while he is focused on the only thing he cares about. Scooping up my messenger bag from our mess of a dining

4

room table, I hurry out the front door and down the long dirt path we use as a driveway. I slow down once I get to the little foot path to the right and soon realize a hoodie wasn't the best idea it being the beginning of summer. I remove my hoodie and shove it in my messenger bag as I continue walking. I will take this tiny winding path through the woods over staying with the king of useless drunken rage any day.

I stroll down the path and allow my mind to wander. Soon I will be able to move out and go to college. I want to study social work, maybe then I can help keep kids from having a childhood like mine. I picture my future dorm room, I will never let it get as dirty as that terrible house. When I get out of here, I am never coming back and I will never be as terrible a parent as mine were.

"Hey Lexie!" I hear Lee holler as he jogs up to me. His bright smile and deep brown eyes are filled with more excitement than usual. The trail winds through the woods and comes out just behind his parents house. "He is drunk early today," I'm not sure how he can tell, but he always can. "You know you can join us for dinner if you want, Ma loves having you around. I was actually just coming to invite you over." We worked out a system so he can just tap on my bedroom window to get my attention and avoid Sir Drinks-a-lot. Even now that we can simply text, it has become a kind of tradition.

"Thanks Lee, what does she have planned for tonight?"

"Tacos, and we have ice cream for dessert."

"Mint chip?"

"Of course," He exclaims with excitement as we start heading towards his house. "Dad is home on leave for a little while." Lee's dad is in the Navy and likes to come home and see his family as often as possible. We quicken our pace, Lee matching my strides. He is at least eight inches taller than me with a dark complexion and short hair. He has a slender but strong build. When we were younger I could overpower him but now I wouldn't even have a chance. His family has all but adopted me as one of their own, even going as far as to include me in their holiday celebrations. Miss Grace Dimka has always gone out of her way for me, cooking favorite meals when things get bad with my dad or giving me the different things I might need. My favorite hoodie is actually one of Lee's hand-me-downs. She has helped patch me up after more than a few unfortunate incidents at home.

"Have you decided on a major yet?" I dare to ask as we head towards his house, knowing and fully accepting that I just opened the door for a long, nerdy speech.

"I am thinking medical technology or maybe early childhood education," he pauses and I know he is just winding up for the speech to come, "I am still trying to figure out which one would allow me to make the biggest difference. I know that if I work with kids I could make a huge difference for them but if I study medical technology maybe I can help develop something to change medicine entirely." He stops talking and looks at me, "am I dreaming too big with that one? Would changing the lives of children be more realistic?"

"You were at the top of our class Lee, with your scores you could probably do anything." At this point we get to the back gate of their large fenced in yard. His dad had added the gate to their tall wooden fence so that Lee and I wouldn't have to risk climbing the fence or be out by the road as kids. Lee opens the gate for me before continuing.

"It is too bad that they don't mesh better, if they did maybe I could double major." He continues, obviously satisfied with my confidence in him and still excited by the possibilities in his future. "Maybe I can still double major, maybe I can find a way to expand upon the difference I could make by studying early childhood education. Children are the foundation of the entire future of the world of course so they should really get more of the focus of change than they have been. Maybe I could add psychology to that and use it to help even more…"

"Lexie! I hope he isn't talking your ear off to badly now is he?" Lee's dad interrupts as we reach the glass sliding door on their back porch. Noah Dimka is the same height as his son and must have been letting their big goofy pit bull mix, Bear, outside. Noah shares the same complexion and deep brown eyes as his son. His expressions seem tired compared to Lee's, likely from age and his years in the military. "I hope you are staying for dinner?" He finishes the statement like a question, knowing I prefer to have an invitation before assuming I can join them for dinner. Bear comes bounding up to me excitedly and tackles me before I can even give Noah an answer. He nearly knocks me over in his excitement and attempts to slobber all over me. Bear is one of the sweetest dogs I have ever met, taking him for a walk has been my escape more than once. I usually leave the Dimka house covered in Bear's gray and white fur, it would annoy some people but I prefer to think of it as puppy confetti.

After sufficiently greeting Bear, we continue into the house. "I would like to stay for dinner if it isn't to much trouble, Lee mentioned Tacos."

"Lexie, you are part of the family, we have obviously failed somehow if you ever think it could be to much trouble," Noah smiles and opens to door for us to go inside.

CHAPTER TWO

Grace smiles when she sees us entering the kitchen through the sliding glass door, "Hey Lexie, it's a little early today. I can start making dinner a now, unless you and Lee have plans?"

"Don't worry about it Miss Grace we can figure out something to do, maybe we can take Bear for a walk." I glance at Bear knowing he will perk up at the 'W word,' his floppy ears practically stand up on his head and he makes a small excited sound. His happy tail wagging even faster than before.

Grace is only a few inches taller than me with a tan complexion. Her hair is dark and wavy, typically it goes past her shoulders when she is at home but she puts it up for work. She has gentle light green eyes and always has a sweet, caring expression on her face.

Lee responds first, "Works for me, I wanted to talk to Lexie about something anyway." Lee smiles and turns to Bear who is watching us very carefully, awaiting confirmation on the walk. "Bear, go get your leash," he commands and Bear takes off towards the front door making happy little grunting noises. We can hear some shuffling in the front room before he comes running back with his leash between his jowls. He sits in front of Lee, struggling to sit still while wagging his tail so fast. Lee pats Bear's head, "Good boy Bear," and clips the leash onto his bright orange collar. We turn back towards the door and Lee grabs one of Bear's tennis balls out of the toy basket near by.

"Dinner will be in about an hour then, be safe," Grace calls to us as we make our way out the door.

Grace Dimka is pediatrician so the Dimka house is large while remaining modest. It has four bedrooms and two bathrooms. I have always suspected that Grace had planned to have a larger family than she ended up with. Their house sits on a few acres of land consisting of the usual Midwestern wilderness and a fenced in backyard for Bear. A few yards back from their fence is the large field that hosted many of our adventures when we were younger. Over the years, Lee and I walked their land enough to create small trails that we often take Bear on.

Bear was a rescue from the local shelter that Grace brought home a few years after they moved next door. Noah was on a particularly long deployment and the house felt empty. Lee spent a lot of his free time training Bear to do goofy tricks and simple tasks. Even with all of his energy, Bear is very well behaved and took to leash training well.

As we cross back through the gate Lee asks, "So what are your living plans at school this year?"

"I will probably just end up in the dorms, I can't really afford anything else anyway. I will just be glad to get away from the drunken menace for a change." I shrug even though I am counting down the days until classes start at the end of the summer.

"You haven't gotten your dorm assignment yet though right?"

"Not yet, I still have to apply." I have a feeling I know what he is about to say but I want to let him finish before assuming.

"Well don't apply just yet, my parents are looking at buying a house near campus for me. They said it would be a good idea anyway, they can continue to rent it out if I want to leave after I am done with college. It also gives me a chance to avoid obnoxious dorm parties. They said I could have any roommate I want or none at all as long as I keep my grades up." We make it to the field and he unhooks Bear's leash. Bear runs around us, getting some of his energy out.

"That's awesome, no dorms for you then," I put my hand out for the ball so I can play fetch with Bear.

"I was actually hoping you would room with me, the house has three bedrooms and two bathrooms. We can have separate bathrooms entirely and use the extra room for whatever we want." I pause thinking about his offer, he puts the ball in my outstretched hand. Bear stairs at it with barely contained enthusiasm, small and silly excited noises escape him as he waits.

"That would be great..." then the realization hit me, "but I don't know how much help I will be with bills. Most of the money I get if I am hired at the on campus bookstore will go towards food and school stuff." I throw the ball as far as I can and Bear takes off after it.

"My parents wanted to talk to you about that at dinner. They said they would get it all figured out and would just be happy to see you in a better situation than what you grew up in." He smiles and nudges my arm playfully before calling Bear to bring the ball back. "Just think about it for a bit, it has to be a lot more peaceful than a dorm." Bear comes running back, drops the ball at Lee's feet and sits, waiting for it to be thrown again.

"That would be amazing but you know I would feel bad if I didn't pull my weight," the words come out as a whine. I want to move in with him, he is my best friend and has been there for me most of my life.

"Well maybe you can work something out with my parents, my stipulation is my grades and staying out of trouble. Luckily neither of us are big into partying, so there is nothing we would really do to get ourselves into trouble anyway." He finally throws the ball, "we might be able to convince them to let us take Bear or get another rescue animal. The only downside would be talking to your dad, you are going to be eighteen next week anyway. Legally you can move out and your dad can't say or do anything to stop you."

"I know, that is kind of the part that scares me. He hates you guys and anyone else who is different from him at all."

Lee lets out a small laugh, "I am pretty sure he hates himself too, I just want you to be safe. If you decide to move in, wait until after your birthday to tell him. At least then if he freaks out you can come stay with us until we get everything all set for the move in date." It would be great to move in with him, to finally feel safe.

"Give me some time to think about it, that is kind of a big decision." I call Bear to bring me the ball and he comes running. He stops in front of me just like he did for Lee and drops the ball. He sits nicely, his tail begins to wag faster as I pick up the ball. "Bear, shake" I put out my left hand and he puts

his big dirty right paw in the palm of my
hand. He never takes his eyes off the ball.
"Good boy," I release his paw, throw the
ball again, and he sprints after it.

CHAPTER THREE

Sitting at the dinner table Grace explains, "I just want both of you to have the best opportunities in college. You don't need to worry about the cost Lexie, just worry about school and food, I will take care of the rest." I want to say yes but I don't want to be a burden. I have always been afraid of letting others take care of things for me. "If you really want to contribute then just work on keeping Lee in line." She jokes and laughs when Lee sticks his tongue out at her. "He might need a little help actually acting like an adult and staying grounded now and then." Lee glares at her from across the table, having just stuffed half of his third taco in his mouth he can't really respond in any other way.

Grace and I get a chance to laugh before Lee can speak again, "So what about taking Bear with us if we did get the house?" it is an obvious attempt to turn the focus of the conversation away from him and find out about Bear.

"Well I don't know about that, I need someone to stay here and keep me company while your dad is away. Bear makes this house seem less lonely." She stops and thinks for a minute, "maybe if you both keep your grades up I will let you each get a cat from the local rescue. You will be responsible for all of the costs and taking complete care of them though." She eyes both of us, "That of course depends on what Lexie decides?" All of their eyes are on me now.

I am not usually this honest about my feelings but there is no point in lying about it here."I would really like to room with Lee. I don't know why but I am kind of nervous about the whole thing,"I respond apprehensively.

Noah is first to respond, "It is a big change, change is scary sometimes. You will only be half an hour away from here if you need anything." His expression is soft and kind, the way I imagine a father should be. "We are talking to the Realtor about it all tomorrow, we are getting the house either way. Just let us know what you would like to do." He turns his attention back to the little bits of food on his plate that fell out of his taco shell.

"You guys have always been amazing to me, I can't ask you to do more." I want to say yes so badly.

"You are not asking sweetie, we are giving it to you. You deserve some good in your life." Grace has stopped eating at this point. She looks me in the eyes and I feel the warmth of her hand cover mine resting on the table. The Dimka family has seen me in the hardest moments of my life. I open my mouth to respond but nothing comes out. They have done so much for me. I finally just nod and meet her gaze. I want to cry but I simply smile.

Grace smiles, her eyes are so warm and inviting. She is the closest thing to a mother I have ever had. She seems almost relieved that I finally agreed, her eyes soften a little. She lets go of my hand and returns her attention to her food. "We are looking at the house tomorrow before signing paperwork, would you like to come with and see where you will be living?" She eats the last bite of her taco and waits for my response.

I clear my throat so I can speak again, "Sure, I will come over before my dad wakes up in the morning." He usually doesn't come crawling out of his room until about noon after a night of drinking. After all that alcohol even he should be too hungover to move tomorrow morning.

"So Roomy," Lee finally speaks up, "when do you want to start packing?"

CHAPTER FOUR

Waking up to We the Kings' *Queen of Hearts* I quietly sneak into the bathroom to get ready for the day. Looking in the mirror I notice that my messy red/brown hair is all collected up on one side of my head. My ordinary green eyes look tired but excited. This is one of the first steps to finally getting out of here. The freckles on my cheeks are a little hard to see unless I am in natural light. I double check that I have a clean towel before turning the water on and taking my PJs off. The warm water feels nice as I step in and quickly start going through the usual shower steps. I barely notice my lavender scented shampoo and conditioner. I shave my legs quickly but carefully, I want to get to the Dimka's early enough to have breakfast and completely avoid my dad. I only notice a hint of my vanilla body wash as I scrub up and rinse off before venturing out into the cold air.

I wrap myself in my towel and can hear my father snoring away in his room. Scurrying off into my room and locate my hair brush. I begin to tame my wild hair and put it into a pony tail before deciding what to wear. After fighting with my hair a bit more I settle on a quick braid, with a hair tie at both ends. I locate one of my favorite tank tops with a puppy on it and an ordinary pair of jean shorts. Quickly putting on deodorant I scan my room looking for my converse and scoop them up on my way out my bedroom door, stopping only to sit on my bed to put them on. I find my messenger bag where I left it, at the end of my bed, and quietly scoot out my bedroom door. I stop to make sure I still hear snoring before tiptoeing across the house and out the front door.

I lock the door behind me and run like a bat out of hell to the Dimka's. Slowing down and collecting myself only just before getting to the back gate. I notice the smell of bacon as I enter the backyard and start making my way to the door. Bear yelps excitedly at the sliding glass door when he sees me coming.

Bear practically knocks me down as I enter the house and Noah greets me from in front of the stove. "Good morning Lexie, I hope you are hungry…"

I interrupt him without realizing it, "poached eggs, toast, and bacon? How can I not be hungry?"

He laughs and adds, "Chocolate milk is in the fridge, grab yourself a glass go and get Grace and Lee after you claim your spot at the table. Breakfast will be done in two minutes." At that I have to force myself to contain my excitement as I calmly go to the cabinet to get a glass and place it at my spot at the table. I have to stop myself from skipping to go get Lee and Miss Grace. I only get to the bottom of the stairs before seeing Miss Grace on her way down. She has her hair up and is wearing a Chicago shirt from their trip a few years back.

"Good morning Lexie, let me guess he sent you to come get us for breakfast." She asks knowingly.

"Yes he did, is Lee still up there?"

"Yeah, just a second," she stops on the stairs and turns to look up to the second floor, "LELAND MARCUS GET YOUR BUTT DOWN HERE FOR BREAKFAST! I BETTER NOT HAVE TO HEAR YOU WHINE ABOUT NOT GETTING ANY OF THE GOOD BACON IF YOU DON'T GET YOUR BUTT DOWN HERE SOON!" she yells up to him in a comically loud, motherly tone. She smiles at me as I laugh, a lot of their family dynamic revolves around messing with each other and giving each other a hard time.

"YOU BETTER SAVE ME A GOOD CRISPY PIECE OF BACON!!" We hear bellowed from his room near the top of the stairs. We laugh as we make our way back to the dining room table. I grab the chocolate milk and almost completely fill my glass before getting Lee a glass too. Seeing where his parents sit, I give him a tiny bit of chocolate milk and place it in his spot at table before returning the jug to the fridge.

Miss Grace lets out a little chuckle when she sees my joke, "I'll do one better," she grabs the plate of bacon and takes one of the crispy pieces. Breaking it in half she puts one little half on his plate. Allowing us to quickly grab a few pieces, she quietly hides the plate in the cabinet before getting her eggs. As I wait behind Noah to get my eggs and toast, Lee finally makes it to breakfast.

"Very funny guys," he says in a slightly annoyed tone, "I know what a pound of bacon looks like after its cooked and there is no way you guys already ate that much. Where is it?" I laugh along with Grace while Noah opens the bacon hiding cabinet on his way to his place at the table. "So which one of you did it?" his eyes dart between his mom and me as he takes a bite of his half piece of bacon. We both act innocent as he takes the bacon back out of the cabinet and fills his plate of bacon, eggs, and toast. We all eat and I fail to keep a straight face as he puts his plate down and goes to fill his chocolate milk glass up the rest of the way.

When he sits down he glares at all of us at the table and Noah rats us out by pointing out the culprits. Miss Grace playfully pushes her husband for turning us in. We laugh a little more before we start acting seriously again.

"We will have to leave in about thirty

minutes, it is about a half an hour drive and our appointment is in an hour," Noah reminds us and I have to force myself to contain my excitement.

CHAPTER FIVE

We get into the Dimka's 2015 Outback,
Lee and I take the backseat. He tries to be
funny and use me as a footrest by sitting
sideways. This only lasts as long as the first
hard stop Noah has to do, when a guy in a
lifted truck cut us off. Black smoke
bellowing from the smoke stacks above his
cab, he loudly revs his engine while
speeding away. We collectively roll our
eyes, we understand that some people love
their vehicles but that doesn't mean they
have the right to treat other drivers like crap.
I hope our house is within walking distance
of campus, the drivers will only get worse
the closer we get to the dorms.

Noah turns up the radio and we continue

the relatively short drive to campus. I focus on my not-so-smart phone, it's a simple little track phone that happens to have a touch screen. The fact that I can get basic apps on it is the only thing smart about it. It was a birthday gift from Miss Grace last year, she drove me to the local store and told me to pick out a phone. When I pointed at this one she asked me four times if I was sure that is what I wanted. She made an agreement with me that if I promised to stay out of trouble she would pay my phone bill each month. She seemed frustrated when I went for a cheaper prepaid card and an affordable phone rather than letting her spend to much on me. I couldn't risk my dad finding an expensive phone though, he would just pawn it claiming that it was my contribution to the household.

I have always had to bite my tongue to keep myself from pointing out that 'household' shouldn't include contributing to his alcohol budget. He is the entire reason I quit my paper route job as a kid, I wanted to use the money for things like food other than instant noodles and mac and cheese. He decided it would go towards a slightly more expensive alcohol than he usually guzzled.

I snap back to reality as we pull up to a cute two story house. There is a small porch and as we get out of the car, I notice what looks like a small fenced in yard in back.

A very enthusiastic woman in a pantsuit comes darting out of the the blue ford focus parked across the street. "You must be the Dimka's," her tone matches every other sales person I have ever met. You can almost see the 'I have to be nice to you but I hate this job' expression in her eyes. "I'm Sandy, we spoke on the phone the other day." She reaches out to shake Miss Grace's hand and then Noah's, "As you are aware this house has three bedrooms and two bathrooms. One bathroom is on the main floor while the other is on the top floor with the bedrooms."

We begin following her up the porch steps as she continues, "All new windows were put in about five years ago, the last owners definitely cared about this house and did their best to keep up on maintenance." She opens the old white screen door and unlocks the weathered front door. We file into the living room, "There is laminate hardwood throughout most of the house excluding the stairs, upstairs hallway, and bedrooms."

She continues as she leads us across the living room into the open concept kitchen and dining room. "The appliances come with the house and while they are a little dated, the last owner reports that they have never had a problem with any of them." She gestures towards a door on the other side of the kitchen, "Across the kitchen is the back door which leads to a fenced in yard. The basement door is just across from that. The basement is unfinished but only because the last owners couldn't agree with each other on what to do with it. The washer and dryer are down there at the bottom of the steps to the right and are also included in the house." She turns to a door to the left of the dining room and opens it to reveal the first bathroom, "This is the first bathroom, it is a little small but does include all of the necessities. The mirror doubles as a medicine cabinet and there is plenty of storage space in the vanity to make up for the lack of closet. The full shower and tub make this a great bathroom for any guests you may have spending the night who you might not want in the master bathroom upstairs." Closing that door we head back through the living room to the stairs.

The off white carpeting runs throughout the entire upstairs excluding the bathroom. "Up here is the master bathroom and all three bedrooms. The bathroom is right here at the top of the stairs," she opens the door as she reaches the top of the steps. "This one also includes a full shower, tub, and vanity but also a privacy door hiding the toilet and a closet on the other side of the shower there." She turns to the next door across the hall, "This right here is the master bedroom, it is the biggest of the three rooms." She opens the door revealing a large bedroom with two small closets and a large window. "The other two bedrooms are slightly smaller, each with one slightly larger closet instead of the two small ones. The one on the right though, has a reading nook with a built in bookshelf." I light up a bit as she opens the door to reveal that the slightly smaller bedroom has a white bookshelf that frames in the window. Under the window is a built in cushioned bench. Lee must have seen me light up a bit as he nudges me. "So do you have any questions or comments?" she focuses her attention on Mr. and Mrs. Dimka.

Miss Grace is the first to respond, "No I

think we are all set, why don't we go down stairs and work on paperwork. Let Lee and Lexie talk about what they think."

Lee and I are left upstairs and he turns to me as the adults leave, "so let me guess you want the room with the bookshelf don't you?" He asks knowingly.

"Of course, and then you can have the master bedroom and we can use the one across the hall from mine for whatever."

"Sounds great, do you have everything you need for your room?" his question makes me pause. I doubt the drunken terror will let me take any of my furniture. Lee must have seen some of the light leave my eyes, "we can look at my house and see what we have extra, I am sure Ma kept some of my old furniture or maybe the furniture from one of the guest rooms for a reason." He smiles and a little relief washes over me. I can't let them do everything for me though. "Lets go down stairs and talk to my parents, I bet they have a plan for that and we can go shopping for all the little things this weekend if you want."

"Alright but if we do I am focusing on the clearance racks." Lee rolls his eyes and we head down the stairs. I am so lucky to have them, maybe soon I can show them how much I appreciate everything they have done for me.

CHAPTER SIX

The Dimka's unanimously decide that, despite my protests, they are going to drag me to the shopping center about four hours away from home. Miss Grace insists that I take some of the furniture from the guest room I usually stay in and that I consider this shopping trip to be an early birthday present. On the way down in the car I make it my personal mission to avoid anything expensive, I get the 'Mom look' from Miss Grace a few times at rest stops when I only get water and some crackers. She grabs me a Gatorade and some beef jerky and waits until we are in the car to give it to me, knowing I won't be able to protest at that point. The first time it happens I get a text from Lee even though he is right next to me.

Lee: Stop worrying about it Lexie, you are practically my sister.

I glare at him from across the car and he shrugs. "Do you want to play the alphabet game?" he suddenly asks.

"You are on," I say before taking a big drink of my Gatorade. I can hear Noah and Miss Grace laugh a bit from the front seat.

"Alright so we will start after this billboard on the right, deal?" He points at a billboard for a fast food restaurant next to the highway in front of us a bit.

"Deal," I pause waiting for us to pass the sign, "Go!" I yell and we both start scanning the high way signs for anything that contains the letter A. We pass one of those adopt-a-highway way signs. "A, adopt," I yell quickly.

"A, highway" he yells at nearly the same time. He spots the burger joint sign first, "B, Burger," he yells and I glare at him.

Seeing an advertisement for a bacon cheese burger we both get caught up to the letter C. The game continues for the next 40 minutes with us getting stuck on the letters J and Q. We both get lucky with a junction sign and Lee gets lucky when we pass an antique shop. He eventually wins when we pass a pizza place just before we stop for a bathroom break.

As we pull over I show Noah and Miss Grace that I still have my jerky and Gatorade left over from the last stop, so that they don't buy me anything else. We all pile out of the car to use the gas station restrooms, this rest stop is cleaner than most and seems to be newer than a lot of places we have stopped on previous trips. The Dimkas have taken me on a few road trips and shopping trips, they always ignore my protests and spend to much money on me. I should be used to it by now, but no matter what I do I still feel bad.

On my way out of the bathroom I see Miss Grace buying two packs of gum, one spear mint and one cinnamon. She always has to buy something from anywhere we stop and use the restrooms at, she feels that it is only fair.

As we return to the car Miss Grace knowingly hands me a stick of the cinnamon gum and we continue on our way. Lee decides it is time for a nap and I have some more of my jerky and Gatorade before popping the gum in my mouth and letting my mind wander.

Years ago the Dimkas designated one of the spare rooms to be mine whenever I needed it, they gave me the code to the keyless entry lock on their garage and told me to come by whenever I needed. They only asked that I leave a note so they know that I'm there.

Over time it became my second home entirely, it is pretty likely that they had planned to give me the furniture from the guest room as soon as the idea of me moving in with Lee was brought up. Given that, I already have a complete full sized bed, box spring, and bed frame. There is also a small desk in the room that Noah brought up from the basement so I could come over and do my homework in peace if needed. There are two dressers, one short wide one with an attached mirror and one taller one, and two small matching end tables for either side of the bed. With the mint colored bedding set, that Miss Grace insists on providing, I actually have everything I would need for my room. She insisted that I come with so she could get me a few things to make the bedroom feel more like mine. While it is very exciting to have complete control over my room and be able to do what I want with it, I can't help but be concerned about how much they insist on spending on me.

My mind continues to wander, making a small checklist of items in my head that I am determined to stick to but I know will only be considered a little bit before Miss Grace adds to it. Before I realize it we are pulling into the mall parking lot and Miss Grace throws a rolled up gum wrapper at Lee to wake him up.

CHAPTER SEVEN

As we enter the large shopping mall we decide to stop at the food court for lunch before beginning our adventure. We choose a little pizza shop, order our food, and seat ourselves while Noah waits next to the pizza place for our order.

"So Lexie do you know what you need?" Miss Grace is the first to speak.

"You guys have already provided a lot of stuff for me, at most I need two reading lamps, one for on my desk and one for next to my bed and maybe a big quilt for the colder nights. Everything else I can think of is just general house hold stuff that we would both need anyway like towels and dishes."

"We will be getting that too sweetie but what about posters and stuff to make the room more yours?" She knows I am going to protest but never listens anyway.

"If you insist on spending extra I would prefer to get some books to fill the bookshelf," I can see the look in her eyes before she even begins to respond. She has a whole list in her head that she just hasn't mentioned yet.

"Well they have a place here that makes beautiful tapestries, you can at least have one of those hanging on your wall. The store that we were going to get towels and plates at also has big comfy quilts so we can get one while we are there." Noah makes his way to us carrying our food. As he sets our orders down in front of us he squeezes his wife's shoulder lovingly and kisses her cheek. Miss grace smiles at him and thanks him before continuing, "We can also get the basic bathroom stuff like shower curtains and soap dispensers there too. Do you still have the warm winter boots I got you last year?"

"Yes Miss Grace, you don't need to worry about getting me another pair." I take a drink of my raspberry tea as I wait for my single slice of pepperoni pizza to cool off.

"What about your winter jacket, does it still fit you alright?" She continues to mother me, I don't know if she knows how good it feels that she cares so much. It may annoy some other kids, but for me it just makes my heart swell a little and I realize how truly lucky I am.

"It still fits me too," I respond before carefully biting into my pizza.

"Well, those winters can get harsh especially if you insist on walking to class. We will have to stop and get you a few pairs of warm socks at some point." She takes a bite of her slice of supreme pizza while waiting for my response. Her eyes seem to smile at me when she sees me roll my eyes.

"You guys don't need to spend a lot of money on me. I really don't need all of these extras." I try to insist, knowing that it is pointless.

"Honey, you are the daughter I never had. Let me spoil you a little bit," she looks at me with those motherly eyes that always get me. If I ever have kids these guys are their grandparents way before my dad gets anywhere near them.

Lee and I finish our food first and he

nudges me before speaking up, "Why don't we meet back here in half an hour so Lexie and I have a chance to look around and talk a bit before we buy anything?"

Noah responds first, "Works for me I want to get a cup of coffee after all that driving," his wife elbows him.

"Oh stop it, you do a lot more in the military than that," she pokes a little fun at him.

"Yeah, but I get to be a civilian right now, let me enjoy it," he laughs and starts tickling her.

"We will be back in about half an hour guys," Lee says before pulling me out of my chair.

We throw away our garbage and put our reusable baskets on their correct return spot before heading down the main hallway of the mall. "So I asked Ma why she never listens when you tell her not to spoil you." I always assumed that she wanted to have a big family but never could. He stops at one of the rest area benches in the middle of the hallway. We sit down and he continues, "Have you ever heard of a rainbow baby?" He asks with a little sadness in his tone.

"Yeah that is what they call a baby that is born after a miscarriage or stillbirth." I think I know where this is going.

"Well my mom told me last night that I was her rainbow baby. I had a big sister, her name was Eleda but she had a heart condition. She didn't survive her birth. I was conceived a few months later. They tried to have more kids for years but couldn't succeed. She had a miscarriage just after we moved in next door to you." I never realized that the reason she didn't have a big family was so sad.

"After that she gave up and was actually heartbroken. When we became friends and she realized that you needed someone it helped her a lot. That is why she wanted to try so hard to adopt you and still wants to. At first she looked at it as fate bringing you guys together, she wanted to take care of more kids and you needed someone to help take care of you during hard times. Then she came to see you as one of her own." Maybe I should just let her spoil me a bit. "My dad saw it in a similar way, he wanted a big family too but more than anything wants to see my mom happy. I just thought you should know why they insist so much."

There is a little sadness in his eyes. He is watching my expression carefully.

"Thank you for telling me, I wish I would have known sooner. It actually explains a lot. It means so much to me that you guys treat me the way you do. I don't know what I would do with out you guys." I can feel my heart swell a little and Lee hugs me. I wrap my arms around him too. The hug is warm and strong.

Once we release he speaks again, "So what colors should we go with for the bathrooms?" He changes the subject quickly with a bit of a smile. I can still see a bit of sadness behind his eyes but I look past it. As long as we don't dwell on the sadness, he will cheer back up like always.

"What about purple for the down stairs one and blue for the upstairs one?" I know he will have more input than most people would expect on this.

"I like both but what about switching them? Purple is definitely higher on my list than blue is. A lot of the blues now are just so plain." The last bit comes out like a whine, he is better at all of this decorating crap than I am.

"Works for me, you know you have a

better handle on this than I do. It is your house anyway." He lights up a bit when I say it that way.

"We should probably go meet back up with my parents." He stands up and waits for me before we make our way back to the food court.

CHAPTER EIGHT

Noah and Miss Grace greet us as we meet them just outside the food court. Miss Grace decides on a game plan, "so, I was thinking we could go to that big home goods store on the right first and then go to the tapestry store I mentioned. From there we can continue based on what is left on the list." She smiles, her eyes darting between both of us looking for a response.

"Works for me Miss Grace," I smile and Lee nods in agreement.

"Lexie and I decided on purple for the upstairs bathroom and blue for the one down stairs. We could look for a shower curtains, towels, and soap dispensers for that first." Satisfied with that answer Miss

Grace leads the way to the store.

Our first stop was for towels, Miss Grace plops four lavender and four deep purple bath towels with matching hand towels and wash cloths into the cart. Next she grabs four sky blue and four navy blue of the same towels and stacks them on top of the purple ones. Next she grabs two soap dispensers both simple and solid colored, one bright blue and one deep purple. She grabs a matching toothbrush holder for the upstairs bathroom and we move on to the shower curtains. She manages to find a purple one with a collage of blocks all over it, each block a different shade of purple. Lee manages to pull a blue one with a similar design out from the back of one of the racks.

Near by Miss grace finds two simple shower caddies. She excitedly takes off towards the rugs and picks out two simple coordinating memory foam bathmats for the bathrooms. It is very easy to see how much she is enjoying decorating the house.

On her way past a display of large quilts she stops in her tracks. After digging through the display bin for a few minutes, she pulls out a beautiful teal quilt with different floral patterns all over. She turns to me with a huge smile on her face, "It would match your bedding perfectly!" the excitement in her eyes is contagious.

"How much is it?" I dare to ask.

"Don't worry about it," she tosses it in our cart and takes off towards the kitchenware. She doesn't give me a chance to argue about the quilt. "So do you guys have color or type of dish set in mind?" She finally stops in front of the dinnerware sets with one hand on her hip.

Lee responds first, "As long as it doesn't include square bowls and the dishes are one solid color so we can match more later, I am fine with it." It is easy to tell he has thought this through. He pulls out a deep red set that includes a number of dinner plates, smaller plates, bowls, and coffee mugs. At the same time Miss Grace grabs a simple set of stainless steel silverware and a drawer organizer.

She turns to Lee, "Okay what else do we need?" her tone is serious and excited.

"A welcome mat, a mat for shoes, and maybe some flashlights to put around the house in case of a power outage." Lee continues, "we will have to remember to pick up batteries when we do the basic shopping for things like pots and pans and such." He shares his mom's enthusiasm.

Noah just sits back and lets them do their thing. He smiles at them every so often and chuckles when they bicker a bit. By the time we check out at this first store we have added a welcome mat, a mat to put wet shoes on, a few reading lamps, a few rugs for different areas of the house, two body pillows and cases to match our bedroom sets, and some decorative pillows for the couch in the living room.

Miss Grace points out that they have a couch and end table/coffee table set that we can have along with the TV from their basement and the stand it fits on. Lee and I settle on getting TV trays instead of a dining room table in a feeble attempt to cut costs. Miss Grace is only convinced when we mention the fact that we would not be using it much anyway so a second hand table from a discount store later down the road would make more sense.

After checking out, we make our way to the tapestry store that Miss Grace mentioned earlier. The store is quiet and small with a welcoming environment. The

walls are lined with unique tapestries of all
different sizes, colors, and designs. Some are
simple realistic designs that look like they
were modeled after unedited photographs
while others are more surreal with an
altered view of a realistic image. I catch my
self staring at a surrealism tapestry that is
about the size of two standard posters side
by side. It isn't the biggest piece here but it is
beautiful. The image is of a beautiful
landscape scene and the night sky. The trees
are distorted and appear unnaturally tall
and slender while the whole color pattern is
a swirling mix of bright blues, purples, and
greens. It all comes together with the
silhouette of a teddy bear sitting at the
bottom of the tapestry looking up at the
beautiful sky.

"That one would match your room really
well Lexie," Lee interrupts my thoughts and
jolts me back into reality.

Grace hears him and comes to investigate,
"Good eye Lexie, would you like this one
for your room or do you want to keep
looking?" her eyes seem to dare me to say
anything about price.

"It's beautiful Miss Grace but I do not
want you to spend to much," she rolls her

eyes at me and goes to speak to a store clerk. After a short conversation that is just out of ear shot the store clerk carefully takes down the tapestry and delicately folds it. She places it near the register and waits for us to finish shopping. Miss Grace picks out a large floral piece for in their dining room, flowers of various warm hues surround a center opening of a bright blue cloudy sky. The tapestry scene seems to match her warm personality perfectly. As she checks out we decide to wait in the hall and figure out where we need to go next.

CHAPTER NINE

A loud crash wakes me up suddenly, my
bedroom is dark and cold. I hear a familiar
female laugh but something sounds off.
Crawling out of bed my feet touch the cold
floor and a feeling of dread over comes me. I
know this memory, I know it all to well, but
no matter what I do I am unable to stop
myself from seeing it. I trip over the same
stuffed animal as I do every time, a small
dog I had when I was ten.

When I reach the door I want to make
myself stop but never can. The light blinds
me as I open the door, the smell of alcohol is
as intense as ever. There is something else in
the air though, something I recognize but
have never been able to place.

"Mommy?" I hear a small voice say as I rub my eyes, adjusting to the intense light.

"Oh great the little brat is awake," I hear my mother slur, "do as you're told and go back to bed." She swings her arm around to point at me and knocks down an empty bottle. It crashes next to a different pile of broken glass. I notice a bright blue rubber tie around her arm like the ones nurses use when they take your blood.

A large hand connects with the side of my head and I fall to the ground, "listen to your mother you useless piece of shit!" my father slurs loudly. I can smell the alcohol and cigarettes on his breath.

"Leave me alone," the small voice screams and I attempt to push him away. I am not strong enough, now I have made things worse. He grabs my messy hair and uses it to throw me into the living room towards my mother. I land on some of the broken glass and it cuts into my arm.

"We will do what we want to you, you little bitch! We are your parents and there is nothing you can do to stop us!" My dad yells as my mother laughs and looms over me preventing my escape. She looks up at my dad and I reach for one of the alcohol bottles on the near by coffee table and manage to grab it. Hitting my mother with it gives me an opening and I bolt out the door. The cool autumn air and my bare feet are the least of my worries as I race to the Dimka's house. Tears sting my eyes, my chest tightens as I run. When I reach the back gate I throw my weight against it, forgetting about the latch. I break down crying at their back gate for a minute before finally opening it and going inside. I make it to their sliding glass door and collapse as tears and emotion overwhelm me.

Bear, only a few month old puppy at this time, yelps at the back door when he sees me. He darts in and out of view and barks loudly. Miss Grace comes to quiet him down and sees me. She quickly unlocks the door and pulls me inside. She holds me and takes care of the remaining glass in my arm. I have to beg her not to take me to the hospital or call the cops. She does what she can and settles that the cuts are not as bad as they could be. She bandages me up and wraps me in a blanket as the tears keep rolling down my cheeks.

"Honey, you know I need to report this. You need to tell them what happened so you

can be safe and this won't happen again."
Her expression is soft. I quietly nod my
head, she scoops me up in the warm blanket
and sits on the couch with me in her lap. She
cradles me, holding me close, while she calls
the police.

When the police arrive they ask me a lot of
questions but it is all a blur. They give me a
teddy bear to cuddle with while I talk to
them. They are all very nice to me even
though they ask multiple times what
happened. One of the officers and a nice
lady stay with us while two other officers
head to my parents' house. Miss Grace talks
to the lady but I never catch her name and
never hear the topic of conversation.
I clutch the bear and the blanket tightly,
staring off into space I can feel the knot in
my chest getting tighter and tighter.
"Honey," the nice lady brings me back to
reality. "Would you like to stay with Grace
Dimka for a little bit while we get this all
figured out?" She asks, the opinion of a ten
year old doesn't really matter but it is nice
that she wants to know my input. I quietly
nod, already attempting not to cry. I hear
her mutter something to Miss Grace about

emergency placement as I see an ambulance fly past the living room window with its sirens blaring and lights flashing. I press my nose up against the window in time to see it turn into my drive way.

My stomach drops and I feel a gentle hand on my back, "come away from the window sweetie," Miss Grace's familiar voice is comforting but the pit in my stomach remains. "Why don't we show the nice lady the guest bedroom with the pretty blankets you like?" I nod and take Miss Grace's hand as we head upstairs. I don't want to leave Miss Grace's side, the thought of having to go back home terrifies me. When we get to the guest room the nice lady writes something down and has a satisfied look on her face.

She kneels down next to me and looks me in the eyes, "Alright honey, you are going to stay with Miss Grace for a little while alright? Just until we get this all figured out." Relief floods through me and I can feel myself start to relax a little. As we make it down stairs the two officers return from my parents'. Their expressions make my stomach drop again. The more important looking officer motions for Miss Grace to come talk to her in private.

"Honey, go get yourself some chocolate milk from the kitchen while I talk to the officers, alright?" I nod and she watches me go before going to talk to the officers.

I have to get on my tiptoes to reach the glasses but I am just tall enough. Setting the glass on the counter I go to get the chocolate milk out of the fridge. I hear someone enter the room behind me and see Miss Grace. Her eyes are very sad, her face is pale.

"Honey, I have some bad news." She gets down to my eye level and wraps her arms around me in a tight hug. Her breath is a shaking and the pit in my stomach gets deeper. She looks me in the eye, "Lexie, your mother was unconscious when the police arrived. Do you know what that means honey?" My eyes drop to the ground and I nod. I think I know what is coming but I hope I am wrong. "They haven't been able to wake her up and she stopped breathing by the time the ambulance got there." She pauses and rests a warm hand on my cheek, "I am so sorry honey…"

CHAPTER TEN

The sound of rain hitting the roof and We The Kings' *Art of War* flood my ears as my alarm goes off. I am eighteen today, usually I would try to make the most of my birthday but not today. Today I am terrified, it's time to tell my dad that I am moving out for college. It's best to tell him, I am not sure what he would do to me if he found me in the act of moving out without telling him. I look at my phone and see a text from Lee from about an hour ago.

Lee: Happy Birthday Lexie!
Me: Thanks Lee, sorry I didn't respond earlier I just woke up.
Lee: No problem, did you figure out how

you are telling the drunken clown that you are leaving yet?

Me: Not yet, hopefully he is still asleep so I have more time to think about it.

Lee: You got this just be careful, let me know how it goes... remember I am always here. I wish I could be there with you when you tell him.

Me: No, he already hates you. I wish you could be there for me too but it would only set him off faster... Thank you though.

Lee: at least keep me updated... I'm worried about you.

It takes some time but eventually I convince myself to get up and shower. As I wait for the water to heat up I can hear my father snoring in the next room. It's a relief that he is still asleep, it gives me more time to think about how I can tell him and keep him from freaking out. I just need to keep reminding myself that after this I will finally be away from him forever. The warm water is comforting as I step into the shower. I won't take a long shower, that would only risk him screaming at me about the water bill. I get right to washing my hair. As the lavender scent wafts up to my nose I contemplate my safest approach.

My best bet is probably to bring up that I am an adult now and should start taking care of myself. Even though I have done that most of my life it might be the easiest thing to convince him of. Rinsing out my hair I contemplate when to tell him. I can't wait too long or he will start drinking and I will be in even more danger. If I mention it too early he will blow up about me not giving him enough time to wake up. I begin to condition my hair as I decide to mention it about two hours after whenever he decides to get up.

While letting the conditioner sit in my hair for a bit I focus on body wash. The vanilla scent hits my nose almost as soon as I open the bottle and squeeze a little bit into my hands. I'm glad I shaved my legs yesterday so I don't have to bother with it today, one less thing to worry about. I focus on how comforting the warm water is while I rinse off. I don't want to dwell on what I will say to much or risk making myself upset. Turning the water off I can still hear him snoring in the next room. The cool air hits me as I open the curtain and grab my towel. At least he isn't awake yet, hopefully I can have breakfast in peace. Wrapping my towel around me, I shuffle quietly back into my room. I throw on a We The Kings t-shirt and a plain pair of jean shorts. I am folding some of my t-shirts into a pile to get a start on packing when I notice the snoring has stopped. The creak of his bedroom door opening confirms that he is awake as he makes his way to his usual spot in the living room.

I finish folding the shirt in my hand and decide to put my wet hair up into a ponytail. I decide it is time to make my way out to the kitchen to figure out breakfast. He is sitting in his recliner when I come out of my room. He doesn't acknowledge me until I am already in the kitchen.

"Going somewhere today?" He doesn't actually sound all that interested.

"Yeah dad, I was going to meet up with friends later for my birthday." He lets out a small chuckle when I mention friends.

"What friends? The only friends you have are that little nigger boy." As the words come out of his mouth I get the extreme urge to punch him. "I don't want any daughter of mine hanging out with those kind!" He starts to yell and gets up from his chair. I can't wait to get out of here. "I bet you think you are going to move out on me soon too huh? You think you are suddenly an adult now? You think you can do whatever you want?" He starts closing in on me, he must have known it was coming.

I back up against the kitchen counter as he gets closer and the words come out of my mouth before I can stop them. "I'm eighteen now I need to go take care of myself and go to college..." I feel his large right fist connect with my jaw and cheek bone. The side of my face goes numb as I fall against the kitchen counter and slide to the ground. I ignore the pain in my back as I try to focus on a way out.

I can hear him yelling, "you could never take care of yourself," his foot connects with my ribs and I hear a crunch as pain shoots through me. His kick knocks the wind out of me preventing me from responding. "You are a useless sorry excuse for a daughter," he grabs my ponytail and forces me up. He is too big for me to handle on my own. I let out a scream and attempt to claw at his hand. Suddenly his free hand closes around my throat. I can't breathe, I can't scream. I try to pull at the hand around my throat as he continues to scream in my face. "You little whore, I bet you are carrying the nigger's child." His free hand connects with my stomach so hard I almost puke.

He throws me against the counter, my back hits the corner hard. I start coughing as I hit the floor, trying to breathe again. I am suddenly aware of a warm liquid coming from my cheek, where he landed the first punch. He winds up and kicks me again in the stomach hard enough for me to spit up blood. My vision goes blurry and I hear what sounds like a strong gust of wind. My vision goes white and there is a sharp ringing in my ears.

CHAPTER ELEVEN

As I slowly wake up, the pain in my ribs and stomach are the worst. It hurts to breathe, as I focus on it more the scent of mint and lavender wash over me. I am suddenly aware of what feels like a light blanket on top of me and a soft pillow under my head.

Opening my eyes I am greeted by soft light pouring through the window of a room I don't recognize. The room is plain but clean, the colors of the room are simple but calm. It's similar to a hospital room but doesn't feel as cold and sterile.

A young man enters the room. He has jet black hair and seems to be only a little older than me. He has a little notepad and pen in his hand. I want to be suspicious of him, I want to demand an explanation of what the hell is going on, but something about him is very calming. When he realizes I am awake he greets me with a soft, gentle voice, "try to stay in bed, you have been hurt pretty badly. I'm Adrian, I am here to check up on you." At this point I realize he has purple eyes, I try to ask where I am but he stops me.

"Don't speak just yet, your throat is bruised pretty badly. You are in Eden," it's like he knew what I was going to say. "You have been sleeping for a while, would you like a smoothie, some water, or maybe some juice?" As he asks he hands me the pen and notepad so I can write my answer.

I write smoothie and as he watches he follows up with, "which flavor would you like? We can manage just about anything here," his voice is still very kind and gentle. I write strawberry banana before handing him back the notebook and pen. He rips out the page with the smoothie order and places the notebook and pen on the table next to me.

"I know this is all probably very confusing for you Lexie, you just focus on getting better now and my boss will be in soon to explain everything. Do you want anything for the pain? We can have something put right in your smoothie so you don't have to deal with taking anything." I nod as the pain in my ribs continues to make breathing hard. He smiles gently with brilliantly white teeth before walking out if the room and closing the door gently behind him. He seems far too perfect to even be human.

There isn't a television in the room that I can see so I try to focus on getting back to sleep. A few minutes after closing my eyes I hear the quiet click of the door. Opening my eyes I see Adrian has returned with my smoothie. He hands it to me and pulls the bedside table closer so I have somewhere to place my smoothie.

He smiles gently, "do you feel up to my boss coming in to explain everything now or would you like to get some more rest first?" I put down my smoothie and grab the notepad 'your boss can come in' I write. I want to know what is going on.

When I finally take a drink of my smoothie it tastes like happiness. The perfect blend of strawberries, bananas, and vanilla.

The cold drink makes me suddenly aware of how sore my throat really was, the cold providing relief as I drink. He nods when looking at my answer and quietly leaves the room.

I continue to marvel at the amazing smoothie for a few minutes before I hear the door open again. It's Adrian followed by a very important looking woman. Her bright blond hair draping over her shoulders, she greets me with a smile that's not quite as gentle but equally as perfect as Adrian's.

"My name is Liliana but most people call me Lily," her voice is sweet and she speaks softly. She has a very calming presence about her. "I run Eden and this hospital. We are trying to help children and innocents who are in bad situations. It looks like we pulled you out of a pretty bad one." There is a sadness in her purple eyes as she says the last part. "We have been watching you for a while Lexie and I apologize that we couldn't come save you sooner. You are with us now though and you are safe." She looks me in the eye and smiles, "I will save you all of the details until you are feeling better if you want but just know, you are safe here. He can never hurt you again."

There is a confidence in her voice when she says the last sentence.

I am suddenly very sleepy as I finish my smoothie. I grab the notepad and write, 'I would like to sleep now if that's ok?' Seeing my response she smiles. "That is perfectly fine dear. Get some rest, Adrian will be in to check on you throughout your stay. Let him know if you need anything." They both get up to leave, Adrian pauses before leaving. Watching to see if I write anything else or simply put the notepad away. As he sees me put the notepad down he turns to close the blinds, shut the light off, and take the smoothie cup before leaving.

I close my eyes and sleep overcomes me quickly. The bed is much softer than any I have slept in before so it doesn't take me long before I start to dream.

CHAPTER TWELVE

"Wow you are a nerd and a mixed boy? You really are a freak!" One boy yells as his friends laugh. The new kid in school stands in front of him.

"Leave me alone," He mutters softly, barely looking at the other kids. His dark complexion is not common around here. He is a little shorter than the other boys.

"What did you say Freak?" They push him, knocking his Game-Boy out of his hands, "I couldn't hear you, Freak." Seeing them push him around makes me mad.

"Leave him alone Billy," I yell as I step between them. I am about a head taller than him.

"Letting a girl fight your battles now,

Freak?" he tries to yell around me. I look him in the eye and shove him.

"Letting a girl beat you up now, Billy?" he stumbles back but I follow him, there isn't anything he could do to me anyway that I haven't already had to deal with. His group of friends freeze, unsure what to do but none of them come to defend him.

"Leave me alone!" Billy yells as I shove him again.

"Isn't that what he said to you? Did you listen to him?" I don't give him time to respond, "so why should I listen to you?" I can see his face turn pale so I point towards the school, "Go, don't let me catch you picking on him again!" I yell as he scrambles to his feet and takes off.

His 'friends' laugh at him and one attempts to talk to me, "you showed him Lexie." I just glare at him in response. Seeing my expression they trail after Billy leaving me alone with the new kid. He is retrieving his Game-Boy from the grass.

"Are you okay?" I ask, trying to soften my tone. He just looks up at me and nods. "I am Alexa by the way but everyone calls me Lexie."

He takes a second to think before

answering, "I am Leland, you can call me Lee though." The bell rings for us all to head in for the first day of school.

We stick together as we head inside, "What class are you in?" He tries to remember but ends up just pulling out a piece of paper with the teachers complicated last name on it. "We are in the same class then, it is this way." I point as we get into the building and we walk to class together.

When we get into the classroom we see our teacher greeting us at the classroom door, "Your desks and closets have your names on them. Put your stuff away and take a seat and will play a get to know you game." He is a very happy and excited teacher, this year should be fun.

We put away our stuff and notice that we are seated in the same row but on opposite sides of the room. I will just make a point to find Lee at recess then.

"Alright class," Our teacher announces after the final bell rings. "Lets play a game called snowball. Write three things about yourself on a piece paper. If you need any help writing it let me know, we are all here to learn. After that crinkle it up into a ball and when I say go we will have a snow ball fight with our papers. Keep going until I say stop and then pick up the nearest snow ball and see what it says. We will go around the room and try to guess whose snow ball we have." He pauses and gives us time to write. One or two kids raise their hands to get some help with spelling. "Alright everyone ready?" He pauses again, "GO!" and the chaos begins.

Suddenly it is lunch I notice Lee sitting by himself, on my way to sit with him I make eye contact with Billy and he sinks down in his seat. "Hey Lee!" I say as I set my tray down and join him.

He seems surprised as I sit down, "Oh hey, I wasn't sure I would see you again."

"I usually end up eating alone anyway so why not eat alone together?" My response makes him smile. "So did you move near by? Someone just bought my neighbor's house, I saw the moving trucks last week."

"It's out in the middle of the woods, one of those weird country roads with a number name." He doesn't seem to remember the exact number. "Do you take the bus home? If we take the same one then it will narrow it down a bit," he adds.

"Bus 16, the driver always smells funny," I giggle and he takes his paper out again.

"Bus 16, so maybe we are neighbors." He doesn't seem to notice my little joke. I push the mac and cheese around on my tray a bit before taking a bite. "Thank you for helping me earlier by the way," he says suddenly.

I swallow before responding, "no problem, it sucks to get pushed around." He looks me in the face and I avoid eye contact by focusing on my food. "Why don't we sit together on the bus?" I try to change the subject, I do not want to scare away another friend, he doesn't need to know about my family.

"Sure, if you get there first then save me a seat. If I get there first I will save you one." He smiles and goes back to eating his food.

Suddenly I am walking to the bus stop the next morning. The left side of my face hurts and I am exhausted but I will keep going like always. Lee and friendly looking woman are waiting for me at the corner. "Hey Lexie!" Lee yells to come greet me, "This is my mom… what happened?" He suddenly asks looking at my left cheek.

His mom looks concerned as she

introduces herself, "You can call me Grace. Lee told me you stopped some bullies yesterday and I wanted to meet his new friend. If you ever need anything feel free to stop by."

Lee is still looking at my cheek concerned, "It is nothing Lee." I have a feeling I will have a hard time getting him to ignore it.

Miss Grace speaks up first, "Why don't you come to dinner tonight sweetie?" I smile at the invitation and cannot help but wonder if she knows. "We usually eat around five so that should give you time to tell your parents where you will be after school and they can come meet me if they want." They won't actually care, I can't tell her that though. They don't need to know how things can be, they don't need to know my family.

"Thanks, I don't think they will mind," I respond just as the bus pulls around the corner and into sight.

"Well both of you have a great day at school and I will see you at dinner Lexie. I hope you like spaghetti and garlic bread." She smiles as the bus reaches us and makes a loud screeching sound as it halts. The distinct clunk of the door is welcoming as it opens. Most kids don't like school, I like anything that gets me out of the house. We smile and wave at Miss Grace as we board the bus and take our seats.

CHAPTER THIRTEEN

The pain in my back and sides persists but has improved. The natural light pouring in from the window is still softened by the closed blinds. I want to figure out what is going on here, I want someone to answer the questions circulating through my mind. Where am I? Who are these people? How did they save me? What do I do now?

As I sit up I am suddenly aware of how stiff and sore I am. Stretching in an attempt to relieve some of the stiffness only makes me even more aware of the bruising covering all sides of my torso. He did a lot more damage than usual. The dull pain in my ribs caused by my breathing is a welcomed improvement from the sharp pain from the other day. I survey the room and notice that there are three doors. One of these has to be a bathroom and it would be great to get to wash up.

As I slide out of bed my feet are greeted by hardwood floors that are surprisingly warm. It takes me a second to steady myself on my feet before I check out the doors. I assume the one that Adrian and Liliana came in and out of is the way out so the others must be a closet and a bathroom.

Opening the one nearest the bed I am greeted by a simple closet containing a small dresser and a hanging rode. The dresser contains two drawers and only comes up to about my knees and gives enough room to hang clothing above it. Folded neatly on the dresser is a stack of light blue towels with basic toiletries on top. Hanging up are two sets of cloths similar to the ones I am wearing. Comfortable, loose, neutral colored sweatpants with a colorful top. The top is tee shirt material with snaps all up and down the sides, likely to give the care staff access to injuries. Upon further inspection I realize the sweatpants have the same snaps, they are small enough to avoid irritation. I grab a light gray pair of clean sweat pants, a purple shirt, the toiletries and a towel before going into the drawers. There are a few pairs of simple underwear and sports bras. I grab the underwear and decide to wait until the bruising goes away a bit to wear a bra again.

I hear someone enter the room and I turn around, Adrian greets me with a smile. "I am glad you are feeling well enough to get up. I take it you are looking to shower?" he asks in an always gentle voice.

"Yeah, I assume the other door there is a bathroom?" I finish the statement like a question and hope it does not sound stupid. It hurts a bit to talk but my throat feels much better.

"Yes it is," He goes over to the door and opens it. "There should be everything you need in here, I see you have already found new cloths and towels. I hope we got your sizes right. Do not worry, it was a female staff that undressed and redressed you when you arrived. Did you need anything else?" he asks and I shake my head in response. It is probably best if I minimize talking as much as I can until it no longer hurts. "Well then, there is a pull chord on the wall between the shower and toilet if you need any assistance or find yourself to be ill while showering. I will get breakfast figured out for you if you want. How do eggs, sunny side up, and toast sound?"

His kindness and consideration make me smile, "Yes please, can I have chocolate milk with it?" I quietly ask as I walk to the bathroom and place my cloths on the counter and towel on the hook next to the shower. I begin to place the toiletries on the side of the tub as he continues.

"Of course, would you like anything for the pain today or do you find it to be manageable?" he seems to think of everything.

"It isn't too bad today," it definitely isn't a lie. I feel much better than when I first woke up here. I don't know what their secret is but I am definitely not going to complain.

"Well if that changes let me know. Take your time in the shower and I will have your breakfast out here in a little bit. I am sure you have some questions so I will stick around and let you ask while you eat." He makes his way gracefully out the door, closing it behind him.

Making my way into the bathroom and

closing the door behind me I catch the first glimpse of myself in the mirror since my birthday. There is a bandage over my left cheek. I pull the bandage off to reveal a cut directly on my cheekbone. Around the cut the bruising is purple but it has begun to yellow around the edges. It is no longer bleeding but I assume Adrian will want to re-bandage it anyway to keep it clean after my shower. My hair is knotted and collected up embarrassingly on the back of my head.

Taking my shirt off I undo the snaps, making it easier for me to remove. The bruising on my back and sides is worse than the one on my face but they have also begun to yellow on the edges. The bruising on my neck is almost all yellow at this point, probably because it wasn't from as hard of a blow as the others. Carefully, stripping my cloths off the rest of the way, I turn on the shower and it quickly responds to my temperature adjustments.

The warmth of the shower is welcoming as I step in, there is a bench at the back of the shower for me to sit on as I let the water gently hit me. I relish in the warmth for a few minutes before grabbing the shampoo and conditioner from the side of the tub.

The scent of cherry blossoms fills the air as I wash and condition my hair. The body wash is the same scent. Thankfully they supplied me with a small disposable razor, I use the body wash as a substitute for shaving cream and take to shaving my legs and under arms. It takes a little bit longer than usual because of my sore back but eventually I am finished.

I enjoy the warm water a little bit longer while I rinse off. I want to know why they are doing so much for me, who are these people? I turn the water off and dry myself with the towel as I get lost in my thoughts. Their purple eyes are so striking, why do they even have purple eyes? I have never even heard of that before. I get dressed and head out into the main room looking for a brush. To my surprise my bed has already been re-made and there is a nice brush and some hair ties set neatly on the foot of the bed. He really does think of everything.

I am attempting to tame my hair back into a ponytail when I hear the door open again. "How are you feeling after your shower, Lexie?" Adrian asks as he places the tray of food on the bed.

"Pretty good, showers always make me

feel better." I respond without looking at him yet, I am still working on getting all of my hair up in the ponytail. As I finish I turn around to greet him. "Thank you for doing all this by the way, why are you guys being so helpful though?" I have more questions but I will only ask one at a time.

Adrian smiles, "Well you probably have a lot of questions so you should probably sit down and start to eat while I explain as much as I can."

CHAPTER FOURTEEN

"So you are telling me you guys are half angel and half demon? And you have taken on the name Nephalem because it is the closest thing you could find in human mythology?" I ask having stopped half way through my breakfast.

"That is about the simplest explanation of it. We also have different abilities based on what kind of angels and demons our parents are. For example my mother is a possession demon and my father is a guardian angel. That gives me the ability to have an influence on emotions and makes me an adept caregiver."

Adrian does not seem phased by my confusion and decides to continue, "Liliana is a granddaughter of Lilith who is the queen of the demons under Lucifer of course. Liliana definitely inherited her grandmother's defiance and determination which is what drove her to found Eden. We chose that name by the way because of the human mythology of the garden of eden. It is of course an entirely different place. God and Lucifer liked her idea to start stepping in and helping abused innocents and children. They helped us to make this place. They are not enemies, even though most human religions seem to think they are. Together they reward the good and punish the bad, it is really quite simple. I suppose if you think about it we are more like aliens than gods or celestial beings."

He trails off a bit before continuing, "We use these stones that are naturally occurring here to see and move from place to place in your world. Different stones have different properties but these are the most common. I know it sounds a bit like something out of those sci-fi shows that a lot of humans love so much, let me know if I need to slow down and explain anything further." He holds up an opaque deep blue stone on a black string that hangs around his neck. "It seems that only Nephalem and few humans can use these to move from place to place in the human world. Most Humans have been successful in using it only for sight. If you hold onto it and think of a place or person it will allow you to see them. They do not work to move around in or see anything here in Eden." I perk up a little bit after he explains it but I don't dare ask for one. They have already done so much for me I cannot ask for them to do more.

"So what is next for me then?" I decide to bring up the more important subject.

"Well, given your age and the fact that you had a way out, we were only keeping an eye on you and not expecting the need for us to step in all of the sudden like that. Your father is pretty unpredictable." His tone is gentle and honest.

"You're telling me," I shrug.

He continues, "Given your age and interest in helping children I would say that after talking to Liliana you might have a few extra options here if you decide to stay, you would probably be a great help to us rescuing other kids. Otherwise you could decide to go back and continue your life living with your friend Lee, of course we would have to wipe your memory of this place and we would have to make it look like you ran away and were kidnapped to explain your disappearance." I freeze when I hear that last part.

He continues to explain, "We can't have every human knowing about us, it makes the most sense to only have the ones working with us know what is going on. Otherwise we risk complete religious chaos, possible breakdown, and even war because of it. A lot of humans are oddly sensitive about what they believe to be their religious truths."

Personally I have never belonged to any one religion. It made sense to me that there was likely a higher power but what did not make sense was the restrictions that each religion wanted you to live by. Why can't we just all strive to be nice to each other and go from there? I decide to avoid opening the religion can of worms with Adrian, "So my choices, if Liliana approves, would be to go back and live with Lee and have a normal life or stay here with you guys and help you rescue children in similar or worse situations than I was in?" I want to make sure I have a good grasp on the situation.

"That is right, or you could simply stay here and live a whole new life here. We have had some humans who simply take care of the younger children who come in here or do jobs just like the ones back home. We have been starting a small society here that lives side by side with the Nephalem in the name of peace and justice for the innocent. Many of the children we are able to rescue do not have anywhere else to go. It is actually rare that you have the third option here." He stops and looks at me for a moment.

I don't know if he can see how bothered I am by this decision. I want to help children so badly, if I can help to save kids from having a childhood like mine, that would be amazing. I can't leave the Dimka's worried about me though, Lee and his family care about me so much I am afraid of how much it would hurt them.

I let out a loud huff of air in frustration, Adrian gives me a concerned look but quickly softens his facial expression as I explain, "I want to help, I have wanted nothing more in life than to help kids like me. I can't leave Lee like this, he deserves to at least know that I am alright so this doesn't hurt him. This is just a hard decision to make." I am so frustrated and there is no point in hiding that here.

"Well you have some time to decide, I will go talk to Liliana about all of this and maybe she will have some ideas for us to make your decision easier. Eat your breakfast, it's getting cold. You should continue to take it easy for the next few days just to be safe." He gives me his signature gentle smile before turning around to head out the door, leaving me to my breakfast and my thoughts.

CHAPTER FIFTEEN

I pick at my food while weighing my
options. The Dimka's have done so much
for me throughout my life, I can't just leave
them. I can't just disappear and leave my
best friend of so many years. This is an
opportunity to make such a big difference
though. The difference you can make as a
social worker is limited to what county you
are in and if you even get the right job in the
first place. Getting a job within the foster
care system would prove to be challenging
on its own even after multiple years of
college. I can start helping sooner with this
opportunity. I can't let the Dimka's feel like
everything they did was in vain though. I
should talk this over with Liliana, maybe

she will be able to help me figure something out.

I shove the last few bites of my room temperature eggs in my mouth and chow down on the last piece of toast. I get up and head towards the door I saw Adrian leave through. My room is on the end of what resembles the hallway of a peaceful family owned resort. A couple doors down, the hallway opens into what looks like a reception area. At the desk is a nice looking dark haired lady who smiles at me when she sees me approach. "Good morning," her voice is soft an gentle. She begins to say something else but a piercing ringing sound cuts her off. Her eyes widen and she hurriedly gets up and leads me towards my room, "we need everyone to head back to their rooms until further notice." Her voice has urgency to it while her eyes look scared.

"What is going on?" I ask as we head back to my room.

"There isn't time to explain right now, I will have Adrian or Liliana come talk to you when this is over. We just need to make sure you are all safe." As we reach my door a neighboring door opens and a small child, no older than three, comes out screaming.

He looks terrified, the Nephalem lady leans down next to him, "Sweetie, we need everyone to get back in their rooms where they are safe." She tries to calm him to no avail, she looks desperate for something to work.

A voice comes over the loud speakers, "This facility has been put in lock down, this is not a drill. All patients please return to the nearest patient room and remain there until further notice. This is not a drill." The seriousness of the situation sets in and I decide that the Nephalem lady has more important things to take care of.

I take the young child's hand, "Hey buddy, my name is Lexie. Why don't you come sit with me for a while until this is all over?" I look at the Nephalem lady and her expression thanks me. I nod and lead him into my room, closing the door behind us. The natural light from the window has been cut off entirely and an emergency light has turned on above the bathroom door.

We hear the door open again quickly as the lady from before comes in with an arm full of toys and pillows. "Here, this should help him to be more comfortable for a little while, there are extra blankets in the drawers under the bed. If the lock down lasts to long then food will be delivered. I will let Deon's caretaker Nephalem know where he is." She stops and looks me in the eyes, "Thank you," she says quickly before she shuts the door and we hear the click of the lock.

The ringing is much quieter in here but Deon is still terrified. He is crying loudly, I decide to try something that I learned from Miss Grace. I kneel down in front of him, "hey Deon, lets go get some tissues to blow your nose and then we play a game until this is over, alright?" He sniffles and nods without saying anything. I grab the tissues from one of the tables next to my bed and help him wipe his nose. I wipe away his tears with a second tissue and ask, "So what game do you want to play?" Instead of responding he throws his arms around my neck in a tight hug. I gently wrap my arms around him, being careful of my healing injuries and any he may have. "It will be alright buddy," I try to be reassuring but I don't know what is going on either.

He is a very small child so I am able to pick him up without much difficulty, even with my still healing injuries. I balance him on my hip while getting one of the extra blankets out of the drawers under the bed. Placing him on the bed I wrap him in the blanket the way Miss Grace used to do for me on bad days. Leaving him on the bed, I quickly grab the extra pillows and get them all set up for myself. Wrapping my arms around Deon, I settle back into the pillows and hum one of the little songs that Miss grace used to comfort me. He cuddles into me as I rub his back, his breathing calms as he stops crying.

I notice the ringing outside the room has stopped just as it seems that he has fallen asleep. The door doesn't unlock and the window remains covered so I stay where I am and let Deon sleep. I don't know his story, but it must be similar to mine if he is here too. I don't know if he has had anyone treat him with kindness before so I decide to let him enjoy the peace. When a kid has a childhood like mine, even a little kindness means more than most people imagine.

I allow my mind to wander in order to pass the time. If I stay I have a very good chance to help other kids like Deon. This feeling, the feeling of helping someone else, is amazing. If I could spend the rest of my life helping kids who have gone through their lives feeling scared and never really getting a chance to feel safe, my life would be perfect. I could have that chance back home but it would be so much harder. Lee would love to do this too, he wants to help kids just as badly as I do. I wish I could give him this opportunity, maybe after things calm down here I will get to talk to Liliana and see what she has to say.

Deon shifting in his sleep brings me back to reality, nothing has changed and I can't hear anything outside the room. I wish they would update us on what is going on. Unfortunately we have no idea how long that will take.

CHAPTER SIXTEEN

The click of the door lock brings me back from my thoughts again. A delicate young woman with a brown pixie cut and purple eyes pokes her head in the door. Seeing Deon wrapped in a blanket in my lap she smiles and quietly whispers the words "thank you," before quietly bringing in a what I assume is a food cart.

I gesture to Deon and whisper back, "do you want me to wake him up?" She nods, I gently rub his back and softly talk to him, "hey bud it looks like it is time for lunch." He stirs and stretches a bit, I loosen the blanket so he can move freely while staying warm.

"Is Gillian here?" He asks

sleepily without opening his eyes.

"I'm right here Deon," the petite Nephalem perks up as he says her name. "It's time for lunch. Wasn't it nice of Miss Lexie to help you during all that scary stuff?" She looks at me while she talks to him. The look in her eyes says everything I need to know to understand how grateful she is that someone stepped up.

"It looks like Gillian brought us quite a few options for lunch, what do you want to eat Deon?" I want him to have the first choice. Even though I am sure they have enough for everyone, I would prefer that he get everything he needs first. He crawls off the bed and runs over to hug Gillian. Leaving he blanket in a heap on the floor behind him. He comes up to about her waist so she bends down to return the hug.

"Well," she begins, "I brought plenty of chocolate milk." She addresses me, "Adrian told me that it was your favorite. We can figure out just about anything you can think of but I brought sandwiches, chips, fruit, a few different kinds of soup, and some juice. What would you guys like?"

I look down at Deon and let him choose first, "Do you have peanut butter and jelly?"

"Of course we do buddy, do you want strawberry, grape, or apple jelly?" She playfully pokes his nose, it is easy to see why she was assigned to a younger child.

"Grape!" he squeals and giggles as she tickles him. She pulls a small bag from the cart and places it on one of the bedside tables followed by a small plate.

"Alright do you want any fruit with that buddy? How about a banana or an apple?" her voice is always kind and playful.

"Banana!" he giggles and she places one next to his plate.

"Now, I know you want chocolate milk, but is there anything else you want buddy?" She leans down to look him in the eyes when she talks to him.

"Nope," he says turning his attention to his food. Gillian pulls a small bottle of chocolate milk out of the cooler compartment of the cart and places it next to Deon's plate. She ruffles his hair a bit before returning to the food cart.

"I will just leave some snacks then in case you get hungry later," she turns to me," how about you Lexie what would you like?"

"Do you have any warm sandwiches like grilled cheese?" One of my favorite simple comfort foods is grilled cheese and tomato soup. It would be absolutely perfect if they had it.

"We sure do, the only choices we have ready right now are wheat bread with cheddar cheese or wheat bread with pepper jack cheese. I have two cheddar and four pepper jack left, if you want a different combination I can go get it as well." Her voice is less playful when talking to me but equally kind.

"Could I have two of the pepper jack please?" Instead of answering verbally, she simply pulls out the two foil wrapped sandwiches from one of the cart compartments and gets them set up on a plate on the other bedside table.

She makes eye contact with me and smiles, "I already know you want chocolate milk, do you want anything else dear?"

"Do you have any tomato soup? That always goes great with grilled cheese." She returns to the cart and pulls a small covered bowl out of the same compartment she retrieved my sandwiches from. She places the bowl and a spoon next to the plate. Last she pulls out another small bottle of chocolate milk and puts it next to my food.

"I will leave some fruit and waters on the table next to the... " a loud explosion cuts her off and the emergency light in the room flickers. Deon screams and runs to Gillian who leans down to hug him. When everything goes silent again Gillian tends to Deon, rubbing his back and reassuring him that everything is alright. Adrian bursts through the door to make sure we are okay.

His eyes are wide but they calm when he sees that everything is fine, "the explosion must have been outside," he sounds very relieved.

"What is going on?" it comes out as a yell even though I don't mean to scream at him. I am very tense and still trying to calm down.

He looks over at Gillian who is keeping Deon occupied before responding, "they call themselves the Anguis," he begins." They have been actively trying to sabotage us for a while." He gauges my expression before continuing. "We are not the only splinter group from heaven and hell, the big difference is, the Anguis believe that there is no hope for humanity. They want to wipe out the humans or, at the very least, let them wipe themselves out. They take everything we are doing here as a direct act against them. They have been trying to attack any facility they can in Eden. Thankfully it appears that our defenses are holding up nicely." He smiles but a flicker of fear crosses his face for a moment.

Adrian makes a quick attempt to change the conversation, "So have you had time to decide what you would like to do yet?" The fear in his eyes lingers but I decide it is best to let him change the topic.

"I was hoping to talk to Liliana for a little bit before I decide," I try to hide the uncertainty in my voice.

"Well as soon as the lock down is lifted I can take you to her, she is usually processing things in her office after major events like this." He smiles and there is hope in his eyes. He adds"Maybe you can meet one of the teams then and that will help your decision."

"Teams?" I wasn't sure what the system was here for rescuing kids.

"Yeah, we have teams of Nephalem and Humans who are assigned to different children and innocents on Earth. They are the ones who are called when something happens to their assigned child and we need to step in."

He watches my expression but I speak before he gets the chance to say anything else, "So there was a team assigned to me? I will have to make a point to meet them."

"You will get plenty of chances, if it weren't for the lock down I am sure Nyyx or one of the other team members would have come and said hello already. Most teams usually like to keep track of their kids." At that moment more light suddenly floods in from the window as the protective shield retracts. "Speaking of the lock down being lifted..."

The over head speakers interrupt him, "Eden thanks you for your cooperation during the lock down. Please see medical personnel for any injuries sustained during the lock down. You are now permitted to leave your rooms, thank you for your continued cooperation." The loud speaker goes silent and Adrian smiles at Gillian as she gives us a thank you nod and ushers Deon back to his room.

"Buh bye Miss Lexie, Thank you!" Deon says happily before shoving a bite of his sandwich in his mouth on the way out the door. I smile and wave as they go.

"Alright, so how about you eat up and we will go see Liliana when you are done eating? I will leave you to your lunch and go check in with her to make sure it is alright if we stop in." Seeing me nod he turns on his heel and heads out the door.

CHAPTER SEVENTEEN

I quickly used the restroom after finishing lunch. Opening the bathroom door after washing my hands I hear Adrian enter the room. "Ready to go Lexie?" he asks in his always gentle and kind tone.

"Yep all set," I quickly notice he is carrying a long shoe box and raise an eyebrow at it.

"Oh, your team mentioned that you wear these kind of shoes a lot." He opens the box to reveal a new pair of black converse sneakers. "They should be the right size, if not I am sure we can hunt down another pair." He holds the box out for me to take as he finishes speaking.

I excitedly grab the box, "They are perfect,

thank you so much." I give him a quick one armed hug, catching him off guard, before practically skipping to my bed to try them on. Grabbing some socks from the dresser in the closet, I sit down and lace up the shoes. They fit perfectly but it feels odd to have a new pair of shoes.

"We can get going to Liliana's office then," He smiles and puts an arm out towards me gesturing that I follow him.

Heading down past the reception desk from earlier we take a left and enter a glass elevator. As soon as we step in I am greeted by a scene of lush green tropical trees and beautifully colored birds. They look similar to the birds I recognize from books, but I can't really identify any of them. Looking down I see what looks like a small commons area with a fountain, a few benches, and stone paths leading in every direction. Directly across the stone path in front of us is a modern looking blue and gray building. With large windows and doors. As we step out of the elevator into the warm outside air I notice a floral scent gently greets us. Looking to my right, I see a large flower garden that I assume is the source of the wonderful smell.

Following Adrian into the blue and gray building he begins to explain, "Liliana wanted to keep the injured kids near by so she can stop in and check on them often. The only way to get in and out of the building we just came from involves various lifts or elevators, we can accommodate just about anyone. Those who are afraid of elevators are simply housed on the ground floor."

Entering the blue and gray building, we are greeted by a large reception desk where more Nephalem and a few humans are seated. Adrian waves in greeting as we continue past the desk to another elevator. We stop at the second floor and are greeted by a large room with multiple Nephalem at different desks. At the first desk by the elevator sits Liliana who looks up and happily greets us.

She reads the confusion on my face, she starts off by explaining, "I prefer to work with people rather than having them work for me. So it only makes sense to share a large office rather than having separate smaller ones. I find it is much better to be directly involved. So, Adrian mentioned that you wanted to talk to me before deciding what to do?" Her voice is kind and her eyes are soft.

"Yeah, I am struggling to decide," I take the seat across from her. "I want to stay and help. This is a wonderful opportunity, but I can't just leave my best friend and the family who cares about me. The Dimka's have done so much for me and I can't just leave them in the dark." I try not to sound desperate for an answer to fix everything but I know she can see right through to all of my desperation.

She gives me an understanding smile before answering, "well, to start off, we can give you a sight stone so you can check in on him and anyone else on Earth that you are concerned with. I can look into some things and see what we can figure out but I don't want you to get your hopes up for anything. I will wait until we have a definite answer before telling you what we can do. In the mean time, why don't you heal up and tag along with Nyyx for a few missions. Nyyx is one of the humans who has made the biggest difference helping different kids and innocents. Maybe a little experience in what you would be doing will be beneficial towards your decision." She smiles and even though we don't have any definite answers, I feel better having talked to her.

"So, I feel good enough to get out of that room. Where would I be staying if I decided to stay here? Would I be able to move in there until I make an official decision?" I try to hide my excitement, I don't want to get let down if I don't end up actually having my own place. I also don't want to make them feel obligated to do anything.

"Well, that actually might be a good place to start. The apartment next to where Nyyx lives just became vacant so we could assign you to that one. Hold on a second while I make some calls." She turns to grab something that resembles a telephone as I try to contain my bubbling excitement.

CHAPTER EIGHTEEN

I try to contain my excitement as we make our way from the elevator to my third floor apartment. The excitement and happiness boils up in my gut as we stop at the second door on the right. Adrian looks at me and smiles. "Now, it is just a small, one bedroom, apartment and we can look at other options if you'd like." He holds a small device over the metal door handle which is greeted by the click of the lock. "All private areas have an entry key like this. You and emergency services will be the only ones who are able to get into your private quarters unless you decide to add someone." I barely hear the last few words as his words repeat in my head 'your private quarters.' I am on the verge of bursting with excitement as Adrian opens the wooden door to reveal a small combined kitchen and dining room. The floors are wooden and the dining room table is the same light colored wood as the door. I quietly wander in as I admire the simple kitchen, complete with a small stove, refrigerator, microwave, and sink. The cabinets match the door and table and the counter tops are a neutral brown.

Adrian lets out a small chuckle, "there is a closet to your right and the bathroom is just after that. Once you get past the dining area there is a lounge area. The bedroom is just off to the left." He seems to enjoy my excitement, allowing me to take as much time as needed to explore.

There is a simple hardwood throughout the apartment and an additional closet and a large window in the living room. The bathroom is complete with a full vanity and bathtub along with the usual amenities. The bedroom is simple with a large window and a closet similar to the one in the hospital. The view from the windows is a simple courtyard with a couple picnic tables.

My thoughts are suddenly interrupted, "I take that as a sign of approval?" He asks,

109

acknowledging my excitement.

"It's perfect Adrian, but where would I get furniture and everything?"

"Well the basics would be provided to you. Any extras you would like would be based on your contribution to Eden. If you decide on this place I can get the basic furniture list to choose from and after you meet Nyyx and start working with one of the teams we will be able to get you some extras. Nyyx lives in the apartment next door by the way. I am sure they will be over to say hello sometime soon. Do you want to look at a few other places?"

"No, I like this one. It is small and I think it is perfect for me." I can picture exactly how I want to decorate this place. I wonder if there is anyway I can get some of the stuff that Miss Grace got me.

"Let me call the housing department and we will get everything all set." Adrian smiles and sits down at the table to make the call on what looks like a smart phone.

Sitting down at the table across from Adrian he pulls up a list on his phone, "so housing is getting everything all set for you to move in here. We just need to make a list of the furniture you would like from the list of the various available basics. Let's start with the bedroom and go from there, sound good?" His eyes quickly bounce between me and the phone as he waits for my response.

"Sounds good to me." He slides the phone towards me so I can see. The screen displays a basic blueprint of the apartment with the bedroom highlighted.

"What size bed would you like? We are able to use any sizing method you are used to. The options that are available that you are likely used to are twin, twin XL, and full." As he states each size he pulls up a little diagram of each and how it would look in my bedroom. Each size would fit in the room just fine and leave plenty of room for other furniture.

"I would like a full size bed, if it isn't to much trouble. Would there be any way I could go get the quilt and stuff that Miss Grace bought me before everything happened?" My chest tightens a bit, I don't want to leave them behind so at least having something from them would make things easier.

"I will talk to Liliana and we will see what

we can do. Position it how you want it on here so the housing department knows how to arrange it for you." He gestures to the phone and looks up at me. His expression only changes when he sees some confusion in my face. "Oh, I forgot to mention, we use this to get everything all set up and the housing department will have it all set for you to move in within the next couple days. We have been adopting a lot of human technology both for convenience and to help the kids adjust easier."

It takes me a second to be able to respond, "alright, I didn't expect that. How about here?" I line the bed up so that it is immediately to the right when you enter the room and allows me to sit on the bed to look out the window.

"And what color headboard and everything would you like? The options are all wooden and are either stained or painted a neutral color."

"The same color as the rest of the wood in here is fine." Keeping things simple will hopefully make it easier on the housing team and it will make it easier on me when I want to decorate.

"Your dresser options are combinations

including a long one with a mirror and a small one for in the closet or a large one and a separate mirror. We can have them be the same wood as everything else." Again he pulls them up for examples and the half sized dresser is able to be placed in the closet like at the medical facility.

"I like the long one and the half. The half one can go in the closet and the long one can go across from my bed." Immediately after I respond he inputs the colors to match everything else.

"I know you wanted to look at getting your quilt from back home, but for now what would you like for your bedding set? We have a couple simple options and you can always upgrade the designs later." He shows me a display that shows a basic down alternative comforter with solid colors or simple designs. I pick out a reversible one that is a dark teal on one side and a mint green on the other. There is a sheet set that matches nicely and a couple pillows. We add some basic window blinds and drapes that match the bed set.

"Perfect so that completes your bedroom. You will also be given the standard of 50 hangers to hang up the clothing in your closet. Moving on to your kitchen, there is a standard fire extinguisher in the closet next to the bathroom." He pauses and looks at me as the excitement in the pit of my stomach bubbles up again. 'My kitchen, my bedroom, my apartment' actually having a place that is mine is extremely exciting. He chuckles at me before continuing, "you will have one of these phones issued to you. This will give you the option to have groceries delivered or you can go to the grocery store. Purchasing groceries and other basic items is on a similar scale as everything else. The basics are provided and you have the option to get more based on contribution. Just to clarify, contribution means that you have a job within the community and are working. Of course you have the option not to and kids who have different medical challenges are given things they can do as well if they want to earn extras. Some kids are on-line counselors or tutors, others help cook in the community kitchens or at the medical facilities. Some simply do volunteer work at places like the local animal shelter. Liliana has a particular soft spot for both dogs and cats. If you can think of it, you can probably do it."

His words open up a whole new realm of possibilities for me. I could quite literally have everything I wanted in life here, as long as I put forth an effort. I can finally be safe and have somewhere to call my own. I can have a pet of my own and not worry about its safety. There is so much potential for me here, the only thing that is missing is the Dimka family.

Seeing my expression light up and then fall a bit again Adrian smiles softly and focuses on getting the basics ordered. "Why don't we start with things like a garbage can? one would fit well in the closet with the fire extinguisher." He points it out on the display, "we have plenty of options but I recommend the metal one with the foot pedal lid. It's easy to clean and empty, it would also keep any smell from the garbage contained." He really thinks of everything.

"Yeah that would work, what about a welcome mat or shoe rug?" I try to remember the things that Miss Grace talked about for Lee's house.

"The basic ones are only simple but we can find something that works. Something in a red or brown would match the wood in here very nicely." Scrolling through the colors he stops and points, "how about his maroon one? It is dark enough that whatever gets tracked in on your shoes shouldn't stain and it shouldn't become obviously dirty."

"That is a good idea, I can get kitchen towels and dish rags to match. Maybe even some basic dishes of a similar color?" I am terrible at this stuff but Lee did manage to teach me a little bit.

"Yeah, another warm color would match really well." He quickly enters a few things into the display and pulls up some basic dish rags and towels followed by a matching oven mitt and hot pad. "I suggest a comfy rug at some point but I would wait to add that until you can get extras a little bit later. We have some awesome memory foam ones available." He changes the display to dishes, "the dishes come in sets usually containing six large plates, six small plates, six cereal bowls, and six coffee mugs. This red set would match everything else pretty well." He looks at me for a nod of approval before continuing, "there are also a few sets that contain all the basic pots and pans and other cooking utensils but I always recommend the 'build your own' box set." He pushes the device towards me, "due to the fact that so many of our kids come from such different cultures, normal kitchen utensils can be very subjective to their background so just check off the ones you believe you would use the most and we can add any missing ones later."

I check off the basic items that Miss Grace taught me to cook with before we move on, "the last thing I can think of is some silverware, a silverware drawer organizer, and a drying rack for dishes."

I hand him the phone and he adds everything to the list, finishing off the kitchen. "So next is the bathroom, what color towels would you like? We can do them individually or in a matching set of the most commonly ordered items."

"Are there any that come with bath towels, hand towels, and wash cloths? I am thinking a bright purple would look nice, and maybe a basic shower curtain to match? And a tooth brush holder too?" I struggle to remember everything that Miss Grace had insisted on when we were shopping.

"Sure, we have a set of towels that comes in purple and has four of each of the towels you mentioned. There is a bathroom set that is a combination of different purples that includes the things you mentioned and a soap dispenser and bathmat so that should be everything. At the end you will also get to choose a list of basic cleaning supplies that will be provided as well."

We continue to order basic items for the living room minus a television. Luckily they do provide the option for a book shelf. The last step is just waiting the last few days at the medical facility before I can move into my new apartment.

CHAPTER NINETEEN

Filled with excitement, I find myself unable to fall back to sleep when I wake up early on moving day. As I shower I run through the plan in my head. Adrian is going to help me get the necessary items that we couldn't order through the housing department. We are starting off with the basic clothing necessities and will move on to toiletries and personal items from there. After that, he promised to help me organize my apartment before getting his next caretaker assignment. I fly through getting dressed, as I only have the basic clothing that the medical facility provides.

I am in the middle of taming my hair when I hear the door open, "good morning,

Lexie," Adrian enters the room with a small box under his arm. "When you are finished there, I have something for you."

I quickly throw my hair into a haphazard pony tail and practically bounce over to him. I give him a quick hug before he gets the chance to hand me the box.

He chuckles in response, "you seem to be excited for the day. Here is the first essential step to being an Eden resident. Provided you decide to stay after all." He hands me the small white box. Opening the box, there is a small phone that looks nearly identical to Adrian's. As I pick it up the words HELLO LEXIE scroll across the screen. "It is programed to you already and I made sure to put my contact information in so you can get a hold of me whenever you want or need. It will probably take you through a few extra personalization steps to start off, but soon you will be able to order everything the way we did for your apartment the other day."

"Thank you Adrian, you have done so much for me." I give him a tight hug. After all he has done, I feel safe enough with him to let him in close.

"You are welcome Lexie. Now, lets get

going so maybe you can start you new life."
He leads me out the door and to the same
elevator as before. This time we take a right
and pass by the flower garden. A young
woman, a few years older than me, who is
tending to some of the flowers waves at
Adrian and stands up to reveal a pregnant
belly. Adrian smiles and waves back, "that's
Sammy, she was one of the first kids I was
assigned to years ago. She met her husband
just after she moved into her first apartment
and now she is starting her own family." He
continues explaining, "humans age much
faster than Nephalem so while she has
grown up, I have only aged about a few
years. Some of our scientists have been
looking into modifying the various powerful
stones available in Eden to slow the human
aging process. With the human-Nephalem
coexistence, there have been a number of
mixed couples who have been struggling
due to the aging difference." Before I get to
respond he is already on to the next topic.
"So, the shopping center is up here. We will
have to make sure to get flashlights and an
emergency kit for you. Every building has a
similar security system to the medical
facility. In the event of an attack, only

emergency lights will be on and all power will be rerouted towards the security systems. The specifics of the attack or security issue will also be sent to every individual affected so make sure to check your phone. You can see the shopping center up ahead, you will be all moved into your apartment in no time."

CHAPTER TWENTY

Putting the reusable shopping bags down
in front of my apartment door, Adrian
hands me the key to my apartment.
"Congratulations Miss Gordon, you now
have a place of your own... More or less."
His words make my already excited smile
grow until my cheeks ache.

Holding the key up to the handle, as I had
seen him do in the past, the door lock clicks
allowing us to enter. Adrian grabs the bags
and follows me in, gesturing me to go on in
ahead of him. Everything we ordered is in
its place. I quickly go check my bedroom to
see that everything is exactly as I had
arranged it on the display. My excitement
turns to curiosity when I notice a small box

with a card on my bed.

Lexie,

I hope you are enjoying your time in Eden so far. Please feel free to use this to check on your friends back home. Come talk to me in my office tomorrow, I may have a solution for you.
Sincerely,
Lily

More excitement bubbles up as I finish reading the note and open the box. A small blue sight stone, attached to a black cord, stares up at me. It's gentle glow is extremely inviting as I pull it out of the box. It seems to vibrate gently in my hand.

"Oh, it looks like Liliana had a special request for the housing department. Why don't I help you get that necklace on? We can then get things put away and I will show you how to use the sight stone on your necklace," he smiles his always gentle and kind smile.

"That sounds great." As soon as he hears my response he gently grabs the necklace and places it around my neck. The cool stone resting just below the dip in my collar bone. I pull my ponytail out of the way so he can tie the necklace and catch a glance of myself in the mirror as he finishes tying it. It is the perfect length necklace for me.

"Alright, you are all set. Lets go get that stuff organized. Just let me know where you want things." Heading back in the kitchen, we begin organizing the various clothing, dishes, and basic necessities all around the apartment. Adrian is extremely helpful in assisting me with getting everything organized and figured out. He explains that laundry is free and just down the hall, any mail that I may receive would be found at the front desk down stairs. If I were to receive something and not pick it up, the Nephalem who runs the front desk would contact me on my phone.

CHAPTER TWENTY-ONE

"I suggest you sit or lay down every time you use the sight stone. It can be a bit disorienting at first and many people lose their balance until they have used it a number of times." Adrian begins the sight stone lesson. I lay down on my bed, on top of the comforter, and follow his instructions. "I will hang out in the living room while you are focused so we can talk about what you saw later. Take your dominant hand and grasp your sight stone, you can keep the necklace around your neck for this one or take it off. As long as your hand is holding it tight, it won't matter." I decide to slip the necklace off over my head and just hold it against my chest. "Now, once it starts to

work you won't be able to hear me or
anything from here, you will be totally
engulfed in wherever the person you are
focused on is. When you want to come back
simply focus on the apartment again. You
will experience something similar to waking
up here." He waits for me to nod before
continuing. "Okay, now close your eyes and
focus on the person you want to check on.
They won't be able to see you but you will
be able to see them. Focus on everything
you remember about them, sometimes a
strong memory makes it easiest..."

As I focus, his voice is replaced by a
different one, "...no new leads on what
happened to Lexie then?" I hear Lee's voice
and recognize the now decorated living
room of his house. Following his voice I see
him sitting on the stairs leading up to the
second floor. "Thank you for putting up
with my calls officer, I really appreciate it."
He hangs up the phone, his appearance
speaks volumes. Stress and sorrow radiate
from his body. My heartaches seeing him so
upset, my inability to reach out and hug him
only make the heartache sharper.

Suddenly, Lee gets up and walks up the

stairs. Following him, we end up in his room where he lays on the bed and dials his phone. "Hey Mom, I just got off the phone with one of the officer's on Lexie's case. They don't have any new leads... I just wanted to let you know... I just... I can't give up on her. She needs someone in her life who won't give up on her." My heart swells, I notice my bedroom door at the end of the hall is open slightly. Needing to get away a bit to prevent tears I decide to go take a look.

The Dimka's put everything in the room for me, they definitely haven't given up on me. The quilt and tapestry are folded nicely on my bed. Boxes are piled up in the corner near the book case. Sitting on top is my book bag and some of the cloths from my dads house. The realization, that a lot has probably happened since I left, hits me hard. Upon further inspection, I notice that most of my stuff seems to be here along with a newspaper dated for a couple days after my birthday.

YOUNG WOMAN MISSING,
FATHER ARRESTED

'A young woman was discovered to be

missing when a concerned friend contacted the police for a wellness check. Upon arrival, officials noted signs of a struggle and alcohol on Mr. Gordon's breath. Miss Gordon was nowhere to be found. Her bedroom appeared to have been torn apart as multiple items appeared to be thrown or broken. Smeared blood was found on the kitchen floor. Mr. Gordon was taken into custody after officials found blood on his clothing. Further investigation lead to information indicating violence and possible abuse within the household. Investigations continue to locate Miss Gordon. Anyone possessing information on Miss Gordon's whereabouts is encouraged to contact the Michigan State Police.'

My heart nearly stops as I read the article over and over again. He is finally getting what he deserves, the truth is finally coming out. Everything is finally working out. I want to go through the boxes and see what all is here but unfortunately I can't manipulate anything. I can only see what is out in the open and even if I focus I can only pass through objects.

I decide it is best to go see Lee one more

time before leaving. Coming down the hall
it is silent. When I reach his bedroom door,
I notice he is simply curled up on his bed
scrolling through something on his phone.
Its obvious he is struggling but he is pulling
through. My mind is made up though,
either Liliana comes up with a way for him
to come to Eden with me or I am coming
home to my best friend.

CHAPTER TWENTY-TWO

Telling Adrian about my experience he stresses that I need to talk to Liliana and should just have dinner and worry about this in the morning. He leaves for the night and I look in my cabinets to remind myself what food we bought that day. All the necessary items for grilled cheese and tomato soup are here, so I put on some blue plaid pajama pants and a black tee shirt before starting dinner. Tonight's plan is to eat and explore the capabilities of my new phone. As I finish putting the first grilled cheese on a plate and realize I have made way to much soup for one person, there is a knock at the door.

Answering the door, I am greeted by

caring green eyes and short purple hair. "Hello?" I ask in a slightly confused tone.

"Hey, I am Nyyx," they extend their hand to shake mine. Nyyx is about six inches taller than me with an athletic build and a confidence that draws me in. Recognizing the name my confusion fades.

"Oh yeah, Adrian said you lead the team that saved me and that you are my new neighbor." I smile and let out a small awkward laugh before shaking their out stretched hand.

"That's me, I just wanted to come introduce myself and see if you wanted to come join us for a little training tomorrow." Nyyx finishes the question with a little animated head tilt and a smile.

"Sure, that sounds fun. I am just making dinner if you want to come in and have some. Its grilled cheese and tomato soup." I want to get to know the person who saved me and hopefully the person I will be working with if everything works out.

"I can never say no to food, but only if you don't mind?" Nyyx asks in an attempt to be polite. I continue trying to guess their age. Nyyx seems a little older than me but not by much. Maybe a year or two tops? Stepping in the door they take a seat at the table. "You look like you are doing a lot better than when I saw you last. How are you liking Eden?" They continue looking around the apartment, probably out of simple curiosity.

"It is really nice here, I want to stay but it is complicated. I can't leave my best friend to just worry about me. He and his family have done a lot for me over the years." I begin making more grilled cheese, "how many sandwiches do you want?"

"Two please. So is there a romantic thing between you and him or what? Not to sound weird, but as team leader assigned to you I did see a lot of your interactions with him."

I can't help but burst out laughing. "Lee? No, it isn't like that. More like he isn't like that. Let's just say that I am definitely not his type." I continue making dinner with a huge smile on my face as I find the thought of being with my best friend hilarious.

"Oh, I am sorry that I assumed. Is your friendship with Lee and his family the only reason you are doubting staying?"

"Yeah, I just used this sight stone for the first time to go check on him. My disappearance has definitely taken a toll on him. I am going to go talk to Liliana tomorrow to see if there is any way he could come to Eden. He wants to spend his life helping kids too and his parents would be great assets here if they were allowed to come." I try to cover my concern with an unfortunately awkward smile.

"Well, it only makes sense that Eden expand and start offering the opportunity for other humans to come to Eden under more peaceful terms." My awkwardness doesn't seem to have an effect. "Liliana is pretty open minded, especially when it comes to anything that would help Eden. So I have been told you might be joining my team if you stay? How do you feel about fighting? And don't worry we are fully prepared to teach you."

CHAPTER TWENTY-THREE

"So, you're telling me, I will have to learn to fight?" My voice cracks a little bit as both excitement and anxiety run through me. I have always had an interest in self defense, mostly because it would help me against the monster who calls himself my father.

"Yes, both in hand to hand combat and in a weapon of your choice. I recommend something that will work in both ranged and up close situations." Nyyx smiles as though it is no big deal. "I started about five years ago when I got to Eden. It is a good skill to have, both for helping to save innocents and to defend ourselves against the Anguis. We only use force when it is absolutely necessary though. We never go after the parents out of vengeance, it would only expose Eden."

"So did you have to use force against my dad?" The question escapes me before I even get the chance to think about what I am saying.

"Jay might have left a few bruises, I will spare you the details of that day right now, unless you feel you are ready?" Nyyx's expression softens and there is a hint of concern in those captivating green eyes. We finished our dinner while we spoke but have been too focused on this conversation to care.

I take a minute before I respond, "I think I am ready."

Nyyx nods before starting, "We were assigned to you over a year ago. The team consists of me, Jay, and Rosa. Rosa and I usually switch back and forth. One of us is always in charge of transport and the other is in charge of tending to the individual we are rescuing. Jay prefers combat, so he is always our main defensive guy. We weren't expecting to have to rescue you. You had a way out and everything was all set up. We were watching and waiting to see what would happen when you told your father and you seemed to have a really good handle on the situation before he snapped. Rosa was in charge of transport, there is usually a flash and a sudden gust of wind. A lot of the time, that is enough to throw an attacker off long enough for us to get out of there. Your dad was one of the few who wasn't phased by it. You were unconscious when we got there. He was in the middle of screaming profanities at you when he noticed we were there. He swung at Jay, who was closest to him. It never goes over well for the ones who swing at Jay." They let out a small laugh and continue to watch my expression closely. "Jay kicked him hard in the sternum to knock him back while I checked your pulse and made sure you were stable enough to move. We were able to move you quickly, it was one of our faster extractions. It took maybe thirty seconds tops."

Nyyx lets out a small smile before continuing, "you were out cold for about a day after you got here." There is a flash of concern and sadness in their expression. There is a sudden, soft warmth in my chest. I am quick to pinpoint the cause of the feeling. Nyyx is showing concern for me, very few people have ever cared or shown any concern. "Adrian took over your care and we were assigned to another innocent. If anything happens when we are not actively watching, the emergency center will call all of the team members to go help."

Nyyx smiles and takes our empty plates to the sink, "Don't worry about that Nyyx I can get that..."

I am cut off before I can even get up from the table, "No, you sit." Nyyx's voice is stern but happy, "You made me dinner, the least I can do is clean up." I scowl and get up from the table anyway.

"We can clean up together, if you really want to help." I refuse to budge and instead grab a dish towel. "You wash and I will dry, simple." My eyes dare Nyyx to retaliate as I drape the towel over my shoulder.

We work on cleaning up dinner before it is time for Nyyx to leave and for me to go to bed. My first training day is tomorrow and I am both nervous and thrilled to start helping.

CHAPTER TWENTY-FOUR

After my morning shower, I throw on some stretchy skinny jeans, a plain tank top, and a brown light weight jacket. I am in the middle of putting my hair in a ponytail when I hear a knock on the door.

A cheerful smile and bright green eyes greet me as I open the door. "Ready to go?" Nyyx seems excited to show me the ropes.

"Almost, we do need to stop at Liliana's office on the way. She left me a note with my sight stone asking me to see her after I get settled in." I point at the card that is now laying on the dining room table. The table is a perfect place for me to put little reminders for myself and there is no way I want to forget to talk to her.

Finishing my hair, I slip on my converse and we are off. I do my best to contain my excitement as we walk to Liliana's office. Nyyx playfully bumps into me as we walk, "So how was your first night in your apartment?" My heart jumps a little hearing the words.

"Honestly, it is going to take me a while to get used to having a place of my own. Even just hearing that it is mine is still exciting." Nyyx lets out a small laugh and their green eyes twinkle a little. "What is so funny?" I give them a playful shove.

"Nothing, I like that you appreciate it so much. Not a lot of people would be so excited about a small, one bedroom, apartment like that." I feel myself blush as blood rushes to my cheeks. "One of my favorite parts of rescuing people is how much they appreciate the little things so many others ignore or take for granted. I suppose the value we put on different objects and opportunities all depends on what we have had available to us in the past." I get lost listening to Nyyx's gentle and kind voice as we walk. "Of course, we do get a few of the ungrateful people now and then. Given the situations we usually pull people from though, they are usually very appreciative of every little thing."

I suddenly realize we are just outside of Liliana's office building when we hear her voice. "Lexie, perfect timing. I was just hoping to talk to you. I have looked into a few things for you and we might be able to solve your problem with your friend. Would you like to speak somewhere more private or is it alright if Nyyx hears this?" She gives Nyyx a little greeting smile before turning her attention back to me.

"Here is fine, Nyyx can stay. So whats up?" the anticipation is killing me and it seems that Nyyx knows a lot about me already so it can't hurt anything.

"Well as I am sure you have figured out, we have been looking into possibly revealing our existence to a few select humans back on Earth who might be beneficial in the advancement of Eden. After looking into your friend Leland a little bit I believe he might fit that criteria.

In order to do this we would just need a little assistance from you though. You would have to help us to decide how to go about this with him and his family. It is obvious that he has a strong connection with his family, we don't want to just break that up or cause them any grief by simply having him suddenly disappear." My excitement bubbles more and more as she continues. Everything could be perfect, I could stay here forever and have everything be perfect. "Of course we will have to look into his family and figure out how trustworthy they are and how we should go about this, if he were to accept. This would also allow you to travel back to Earth and get some personal items if you'd like." She pauses and lets out a small laugh as she sees my excitement bubbling more and more. "This will all depend on how the next few parts of the process go and if he accepts. It all does look very promising though."

I want to hug her but I resist the temptation. "That would be wonderful Liliana, thank you so much for looking into this."

Her kind eyes meet mine and she continues, "Well, we will look into it more after you do some training with Nyyx. Adrian gave me the number to contact you with and I will call you when the next step of the process is ready. I need to get a few things done right now though so enjoy training."

"Thank you again Liliana, I will talk to you later." She nods and takes off back towards her office.

CHAPTER TWENTY-FIVE

"Now keep your hands up and make sure your first two knuckles are hitting the bag," Nyyx gives me instruction as I work on my hand to hand combat form for the first time in my life. I punch the bag again, remembering to breathe with each punch. "Good, you have power behind it, we just need to make sure you can execute the moves effectively and avoid getting hurt." They have been picking on me, little by little, the entire time we have been training. Surprisingly enough I actually enjoy it. It's a lot like the Dimka family dynamic I have always admired so much. There is something about how playful Nyyx is about everything that makes heart jump and forces me to smile. "We can take a break soon, the team should be here in a little bit so you can meet them. I don't know if you want to be all gross and sweaty when you finally meet them," Nyyx jokes around a little and a punch them in the shoulder. Only upon punching Nyyx to a realize how solid they are and how strong they must be.

A wave a mild embarrassment washes over me, I should have assumed that anyone who is part of a rescue team would probably be in really good shape with all of the necessary training. "Maybe I can meet them over lunch? I can't train all day, I do need to eat."

"Lexie we have been here for twenty minutes how can you already be hungry?" I groan realizing that Nyyx is right. We have only been in this over sized training facility for about twenty minutes. I love food though I can't help it, now that it is so readily available I want to try new recipes and see what I have missed out on only eating good meals with the Dimkas.

"I can't help it! The food here is so good and I want to cook more. You know there wasn't much for me to eat growing up, unless I was at the Dimka's."

"I know, I am just giving you a hard ti…" Nyyx is cut off by a piercing alarm. Red lights flash and Nyyx immediately pulls me towards a near by room.

Locking the door behind us we hear a voice over the loud speakers, "TAKE SHELTER IN THE NEAREST SAFE HOUSE. WE ARE UNDER ATTACK. THIS IS NOT A DRILL." The message repeats twice before leaving only the piercing sound of the alarms for us to listen to. A loud explosion shakes the building and people can be heard screaming outside. Nyyx and I camp out in the corner of the room, waiting for all of this to end.

"We should be safe here, there is at least one safe house like this in every building in Eden. There are also a couple bunkers in different outdoor locations like parks and conservation areas." Nyyx tries to smile but there is obvious fear behind it. "The Anguis attacks never last more than a few hours… So are you planning on staying now that we are working on getting your friend the opportunity to come here?" Nyyx's attempt to distract me doesn't fool me but given the situation, it's best not to call them out on it.

"Yeah, I think I could be really happy

here."

"Well, what is the first thing you want to do once you have been a part of the team for a while?"

"I want to visit the animal shelter that Adrian mentioned. I have always wanted to get a cat but feared for its safety to much to get one when I was younger."

"I actually had the same idea when I got here too. I have a small, deaf, gray cat named Stormy. She is a sweetheart and was rescued when a useless piece of crap tried to drown her after finding out she is deaf. I will never understand the mindset of some people."

"Poor thing, well I'm glad she has you now." There is a loud bang outside the room and both of us immediately focus on the door. All memory of our previous conversation fades as we prepare for the worst. Nyyx moves between me and the door.

We begin to hear shouting from the other side of the door, "Collect all of the useless vermin you find!" the faceless voice booms. The sound sends silent chills down my spine. Is that one of the Anguis? Is that what they think of humans? Suddenly

something hits the door hard but the door
maintains its place.

A small wave of relief runs through me
seeing that the door hasn't budged.
Suddenly it happens again, and again. The
bang getting louder and louder each time.
As suddenly as it started it stops, followed
by a quiet beeping. The beeps grow louder
and louder until a loud explosion fills the
room. Dust blinds us as we try to prepare to
defend ourselves. Ears ringing, eyes
stinging, and lungs caked with dust; our
attempts to even get our bearings fail. I am
suddenly struck in the stomach and then in
the side of the head as I lose my balance and
everything goes dark and quiet.